An Imperfect Fortress

An Imperfect Fortress

Scott Guy

With contributions by Rachel Ohmes

And

Jessica Whittamore

**Picture contributions by Mark Kucza
And
Shannon Garrett**

Scott Guy
2014

First Printing: 2014

ISBN 978-0-692-30709-0

Dedication

To my family and friends:

Thank you for your support and patience through all of the drafts and iterations of these stories.

Contents

Introduction

This anthology is a collection of four short stories and one novel-length tale. It has been designed to allow the audience to enjoy each story for its own merits or, once every story is read, to understand the broad scope of the book's mosaic composition.

Rarely satisfied with conventionality, I had challenged myself to write each story in some unique fashion, each helping to enhance the feeling of the individual entry. Be it through genre, general format or pace; each story has been meticulously crafted to offer something to the audience that is unique from the others herein.

An Imperfect Fortress

CHARLES IN THE HOUSE OF MR. GREENE

An Imperfect Fortress

Charles was the name they gave me. 'They...' I don't even know who I'm talking about. Everyone used to tell me Charles was an unusual name...I never cared, but I guess I never really took the time to care. Charles is all I'd answer to. 'Charlie,' 'Chuck,' I just don't see me as fitting in with any of those nicknames, or rather, any of those names fitting in with me. Charles it was, Charles it stayed, and that is all it said on my grave-marker: Charles.

As that last bit hinted at: I'm already gone from this world. I wish I could tell you that my death meant something to someone, or that I went down fighting for some great cause or any number of epic and meaningful phrases, but the truth is I just didn't see the other car coming.

My tombstone (as you may have realized) was missing quite a bit of information. There were no kind or wise words etched into granite, no dates of birth or expiration, so you'll have to forgive me for not being able to fill you in on the details. Truth of the matter is I don't know all the details, what years I existed in, I don't know my beginning and end dates, just the events in between. Truth of the matter is, there are some folks out there who would have you believe my life was cut short, but to be honest, I never saw that way at all; time just moves differently for everyone I suppose.

Injustice followed me into this world, and with injustice I grew into my first memories. Mine was actually a multiple birth, there were two of us. I was the first to come out. I had a younger sister for a few moments in time. I remember some of her qualities, others I do not, each for different reasons, but at least I remember the reasons...and that is enough for the purposes of the story. While I don't believe that we were born in prison, I believe I had been put there to pay for the crimes of my mother, who also died shortly after giving birth.

The younger of us was born barely alive, though I guess you could say that about any newborn. What I meant to say was that the youngest would never have been able to thrive, and if given the chance to do so on her own, she would have died within minutes after coming out of our mother. I don't know why she did it, killed her I mean, perhaps my mother didn't want to see her suffer, perhaps she knew that she didn't have long to live either, but she ended my sister's short existence. For that, my dying mother's crimes, they took me, the only thing left of her in this world, and locked me up. And that is how my life began.

I grew up in my cell, watching the other inmates writhe and age in their uniquely grotesque manners, hoping that one day they would come and tell me that I had fully paid my mother's debt, and that I would be free to leave. There would be nights that I would lay awake dreaming, wondering what life was like outside of my tiny cage and my 15 minutes of exercise. Daylight would break over those nights and the realizations would come back to me. The realizations that people only left here for two reasons: they were going home, or they were being put to death.

Some days would be better than others. Some days all of the faces would be the same, everyone still there from the day before. Other days would bring new faces or see old faces leave. Occasionally there would people walk by that I had never met, people that had no business being where they were; people that would never be locked away. Sometimes they would stare, sometimes they would point, others would waive as if to mock us. I was largely avoided, but once in a great while would be tossed a glance, be it one of pity, concern or fear.

I imagine there are some folks out there that have no reason to believe they will ever have to stay in a place like this, and so they come to see what it is like for those of us who are stuck. Perhaps it's silly seeing someone like me, relatively young and bound to this cell. Maybe it strikes them as a tragedy, not that they would know my story, or even give me a second thought once they were safely away. I am sure that the frightened response is brought to the surface by the noise that bombards these close walls whenever visitors do come. The deafening and profane howls echoing in the heads of those who sought to bring us hope, or at the very least, the knowledge that freedom still existed for some.

I would eventually be freed. There were several conditions, none that had ever been read or told to me, but conditions I would eventually learn through painful experience. To recount the day of my freedom I imagine I was the only one that had no idea of what was going on. The day had started just as any other, in fact it was relatively early in the day that the guard came to me and said almost quizzically:

"Charles?"

I don't know what kind of response he was looking for, so I lumbered up to the bars and looked down the hallway in the same direction as the guard. I would jot my eyes at the face of the guard and then back down the long corridor, waiting to see what was coming, fully anticipating that I was about to be put to death. With those moments came a memory of something another inmate had once told me:

"…the key to dying without fear is knowing that no one will care that you're gone."

I suppose by that reckoning I should not have been as afraid as I had been, no one had ever loved me, but still I found my throat tight with fear and anxiety. Perhaps that fear came from not knowing what was happening, and maybe that fear would have gone away if they had simply told me I was being put to death, that would have book-ended things for me a bit better than staring expectantly down that hall.

Toward me he came and for the first time in my life I laid eyes on Mr. Greene, the man whose custody I was to be released under. Mr. Greene was a tall man, much taller than I could ever have hoped to be, even at my best. He smiled and seemed friendly enough, and from time to time that smile would fade, but I knew that it always would return if I just waited long enough. He was clean and well-dressed; a man who cared for his-self enough that he could be trusted to take care of another. He looked down at me, said my name with a stern but welcoming tone and I walked with him for the first time toward the outside gate.

Mr. Greene kept me close as we loaded into his car. He opened the door to the backseat for me as he would go on to do countless times.

He walked around the rear of the car and made his way into the driver's seat. Before starting the vehicle he turned to me and with that smile on this face said to me:

"Let's go home."

Those next few days were full of learning for me. To look back on it everything seems so basic and mostly sensical. Mr. Greene was never one to waste words with me. When he spoke he spoke directly and in short statements, rarely asking questions.

"This is where you will eat," or "This is where you will sleep."

Mr. Greene's home was large and beautiful, well kept, rarely disorganized or dusty. He maintained the inside and outside of his house with precision. His lawn would never grow too wild in the spring and summer, never too filled with foliage or snow in the other months. I remember Mr. Greene's home as being the first place I would ever feel truly comfortable. For all of its splendor, there was one facet of the house that I did not care for: his cat.

Mr. Greene never seemed to me to be the type of man to enjoy the company of felines, but he never owed me an explanation to its being there and I would never ask. Whiskers was a cat that had not aged well, from the looks of her I would have estimated her age to 80. Patches of fur were either missing or knotted to the point of derangement. Her eyes never matching position, one always open, one always shut, as if she had forgotten or simply didn't have the energy to maintain them both at the same time.

I had made the effort to befriend Whiskers at our first introduction; an act that was met with hissing and clawed swipes at my nose. From that day I knew it would just be a waiting game. I would avoid Whiskers as best as possible and wait for that wonderful day to come when Mr. Greene would bury that cat in the backyard, look down at me and say:

"This is where we bury pets."

I found myself fighting to fend off a smile as I stared down at the grave-marker, proudly marking the cat's final resting place: Whiskers.

Mr. Greene was a perfectly likeable man, though from time to time he did lose his temper. From what I had gathered from overheard telephone conversations, Mr. Greene was a widower. He lost his wife weeks before his daughter was to leave for college, making it all the more difficult when she left and all the more important for him to encourage her to leave. It had been more than a couple of months since his wife's passing that he joined the program which would allow our paths to cross.

I imagine he felt incredibly alone; losing both his wife and parting with his daughter. I imagine that my being here in his house is an attempt to fill that loneliness. Why he chose to bring someone like me here instead of taking up some sort of hobby or the like is beyond me, but I was grateful. While we never did become best friends (as I believe he had hoped for), there were plenty of nights shared in front of the TV, watching anything from sports to news to comedies depending on Mr. Greene's mood that day.

He was a perfectly likeable man, though from time to time his emotions would get the best of him and I would hear him cry openly. Even if I were in the room; to look at him you would assume he was completely alone. Sometimes, if he were sad or lonely enough, he would ask me to keep him company as he fell asleep. On those nights I would stay in his room, resting in a chair near his bed, making sure his tears would eventually stop as he drifted off. There would be times he would cry, times he would scream, times that he would be mad or even occasionally strike me for reasons that are still very unclear. I never seemed to mind though, the physicality that is, and I never retaliated; not once.

Mr. Greene's daughter was the center of his universe. Her name was Saundra and never before had I encountered a father as proud of his daughter, limited as though my experiences may have been. She would come and go as she needed. I do not know exactly how far away her school was, or what motivated her visits, but whenever she left us I never assumed she would be coming back.

Between the two, Mr. Greene and his daughter, I would say that I preferred her company. There was something to her, something basic that I connected with. She was pretty but not beautiful, sincere yet aloof, plain but still somehow unforgettable. She was comforting to me in ways that I had never experienced before. For a time, happiness for me was hearing her say my name. I would lay near her, like her father, until she fell asleep, and then I would retire for my night to where Mr. Greene had originally instructed. When she was gone, I would open the door to her room slightly at nights and remember how peaceful she would look lying in her bed and wish that I could see her again. She is the first person that I can say I have ever missed.

Saundra did return to us one day, and for a long while, she stayed with us. As the months passed she grew more and more pregnant. During this time Mr. Greene devoted the majority of his attentions to her, tending to her every need. He would watch with pride as his daughter's belly would grow and eventually learn to kick. He remained patient with her through her moodiness and late-night cravings, perhaps constantly reminding himself of the blessing of having any family at all. I remained a loyal friend to both Mr. Greene and Saundra as the new child, a girl, was born prematurely into the world.

Perhaps it was some latent memory from birth of my weak sister's death, but some unnamed emotion arose in me when that baby was born. As much as I had grown to love Saundra, I had become suspicious of her, believing that she may not desire to keep a child as frail and weak as Grace. I found myself staying in the bedroom with Grace, remaining close enough to be certain that no harm would come to her and still distant enough to elude any suspicion of my vigilance.

As Grace began to grow and develop into a stronger, healthier child, a new but familiar rhythm returned to Mr. Greene's household. Grace caught up to the normal standards for a child, never developing any sort of illness or impairment. I, however, remained as close to her as possible, coming to love her even more so than I had Mr. Greene or Saundra.

Mr. Greene took advantage of every opportunity to be affectionate with both this daughter and granddaughter. He took his calling as Grace's primary male role-model very seriously, making sure that she knew how loved she was, and that she was the spitting image of her grandmother. Mr. Greene grew to struggle with silence, having gotten used to the company of commotion. Often times he would talk to himself, or talk to his dead wife in order to stifle the silence whenever the house was otherwise empty. He would tell her all about her namesake and how privileged he felt just to watch her grow. Our friendship was possibly the only thing to remain unchanged in that house. Mr. Greene and I remained friends as we always had, though he would never let me forget that I was not part of the family, and merely there out his generosity. He never seemed to mind my close relationship with his granddaughter, though he did watch me closely during her formidable first weeks.

Saundra eventually found herself a good-paying job and would be gone for several hours out of the day. Though she had moved into the house with me and Mr. Greene, part of me retained the fear that one day she would simply not return, and I treated each parting as the final farewell. I am glad to say that, for as long as I had been alive, Saundra continued to come home to us, and that homecoming would be the highlight of everyone's day.

As the years went by and Grace approached the age required to go to school, the family and I would move outdoors to the front yard on sunny days. Mr. Greene had hung a tire swing from the giant oak in anticipation of the day that he would be able to push his little girl's little girl. Saundra bought as many adorable dresses for Grace as she could find, and would dress her in them as often as possible knowing that Grace would soon outgrow them.

The day of my death was actually quite nice. Saundra had returned from work early in the day and we returned once again to the front yard, running and rolling and playing with the child. I remember vividly the vehicle turning down our street and sensing somehow that something bad was about to happen. As the other three continued romping around in the grass, I stood now motionless as I watched the backseat window of the sedan descend. As the car passed, a young teenage boy hung himself out of the window, hurling a number of water-filled balloons at Mr. Greene, Saundra, and Grace. As one of the rockets made contact with Grace, she was knocked over, unhurt but scared and crying as loud as she knew how.

As Mr. Greene took inventory on the family to ensure everyone had remained uninjured, I knew that he would not have time enough to gather his thoughts and react to this wild act of vandalism. Within just a few heartbeats I began chasing the car, bounding ever faster toward the punks that would dare bring any fear to that precious child. As I had made it nearly a block from the house before Mr. Greene had noticed, I could only hear faintly his distressed calls for me to come back. Those calls would remain unheeded as I drew closer and closer to the perpetrators, not knowing exactly what it is I would do when I caught up to them.

I gave those boys quite a scare and followed them an impressive number of blocks before rounding a corner onto one of the busier neighborhood streets. With that left turn came another car, the unseen car that I had mentioned before. The boys in the car continued on their way unhindered, not stopping to observe the carnage. In fact the car that hit me only stopped long enough for the driver to make sure no major damage had been wrought upon his SUV.

Mr. Greene was the one who found me, though I am sure he was the only one who was looking. Just as the day he came and brought me home from that prison, he bent down and gathered me in his arms and said;

"Let's get you home."

I died before making it back. I was never able to say my goodbye's to the girls that had made their way into my heart, nor was I ever able to express my gratitude to the man that gave me a chance at life. Still, as I lay bleeding in the arms of Mr. Greene, I remembered the words of that inmate from years past:

"…the key to dying without fear is knowing that no one will care that you're gone."

At that moment I realized that I respectfully disagree with those words. Even though I was not able to say to that family the things in my heart, that I was grateful for their affections, I was dying without fear because they knew that I loved them more than anything else in the world.

As Mr. Greene returned home that day with my lifeless body in his arms, my blood on his shirt, and tears in his eyes, he took care to make sure that Grace would not be exposed to such a mess. It was probably little more than an hour's time that was taken to put me in the ground. The three of them gathered; Mr. Greene, Saundra, and Grace, looking down at that headstone that simply read "Charles," laid to rest right beside Whiskers the cat.

SCRAP LORDS

To say 'a war was brewing' would have been accurate 7 years ago, 'least that's how Tribe would have put it. As of today, that war has been raging under the weathered skin of our town, burning at the system of order that had up to this point maintained Reason as Ruler Sovereign.

We were such a quiet town for having such big-name stores. To look at it now, the notion of quiet seems lost to the days when kids walked freely down the street to the soda shop, t.v. existed in only three channels, everyone knew someone named Ma or Pa, and life itself seemed to exist solely in sepia tones. That was our town, quiet, peaceful, and downright pleasant.

There we were, our quaint existence right in the middle of nowhere, usually between where you was coming from and where you were heading. That's actually all you need to know about how we came into having those big, brand name shops I was talking about. Those trifold brochures the state puts out would have you believe us to be a 'bustling' community; a stretch even on our busiest day.

Perhaps, though, the greatest misnomer would be name you learnt in history class. Text books put our town cradled in the middle of 'The Great Plains.' For any of you who have taken the time or had the misfortune of driving though these parts, you know that they aren't too great, but they sure are plain…so we can settle for half-right at least.

Things have changed here for the residents; sure people still drive through, people that don't know and have no reason to know what went on, people that have no idea as to what happened.

The memories of man are limited. Concepts of time and events, even local politics are fleeting things that disappear just as quickly as the winds can sweep them away. But the memories of a town, the memories of history are lasting, unforgiving things, often as ruthless as the men (in this tale at least) that have etched their names into the indelible stones of time.

Bishop; that was his name, just those letters and nothing more. A gruff, middle-aged man; once a nobody and content to have stayed that way. Though for this man it seems fate would not have allowed such a mundane existence. For 50-some-odd years Bishop's DNA was that of the town's: old, rundown and dusty. For as long as anyone in the town could remember, the Bishop family had lived here. Hell, one of Bishop's great great great great great relative's could've settle the town. I suppose that would've been one of his great great gr…well…shoot, you get the idea. Bishop was born and raised here. After his dad passed on, Bishop took on the duties as the town's scrap metal collector. He was the man in town that had the old metal signs in his yard from brands of detergent soap and soda pop. He would go around the town, searching from this neighborhood to that one, scrounging around for scrap metal, old rusted car or appliance parts, things like that, and he would take them to the local recyclery for his daily allowance.

Loner as he is now, Bishop tried his hand at a domestic life, but that was 30 years ago. He had a wife, a woman he pulled in to his meager existence, a woman that left Bishop soon after finding out she was pregnant. Bishop came home one day, as the story goes, with only a note that read something like "You damned old man, you ain't never gonna change, I'm gone, we ain't comin' back."

That was it. I don't imagine that Bishop has said much to anyone since that day. To look at him you would think his life ended at that exact moment in time. Why he continued to wake up, to work, to clean or bathe or exist if ever he really did at all would rank up there with the other great mysteries of the world.

Then, about seven years ago, Tribe showed up in town. Mathias Tribe, a good-looking man in his early thirties. A clean-cut, squared jaw, muscular man that cared for his-self and knew how good he looked in a suit, a man whose reputation as a former killer preceded his arrival to our town. Why he showed up is still an enigma, maybe it was to get away from that life, maybe it was to go somewhere and find his past, who knows. I guess you could ask him, Tribe, I mean, but I have never known anyone to just ask that man a question that wasn't motivated by favors or money.

So after only a few weeks of living in the town, Tribe decided he would enter into the scrapping business, a business with very limited competition, just one old and rusted man: Bishop.

Now, I don't know exactly what transpired between these two very different men during their limited meetings, but each must have stood their ground. On one hand you had Bishop, a dusty and near-ancient mound of a man, and on the other you had Tribe, a new and shiny tower of speculation, but after a month's time it seemed as though the lines had been drawn, territories marked, one man would no longer encroach on the others. How they both grew or maintained their limited businesses to stability is beyond me, but that is how it was, again, for a time.

The memories of man are fleeting, tiring things, but the town, history, continues, lasts, remembers.

Now with these characters in place, living quietly and amicably, the fates threw in yet another group, a crude gang of boys just old enough to drive; cruel, intolerable, unloved boys, three of 'em…two brothers and a friend. The older of the two brothers was the leader of the crew, he was the brains, the vicious intellect that kept the gang together, and his name was Malice. His younger brother, the timid and effeminate Hue, always cowering under the wing of his brother, peeking out only to laugh at whatever torturous acts were being played on any of unnamed victims. Any emotion that wasn't driven by anger, hatred, fear or lust existed only between these two. The third member of the gang was Georgie, he was the muscle, his actions carried out swiftly once ordered from Malice, without question, without hesitation, without care.

A storm heralded the arrival of the gang, black clouds hanging low in the sky over the town, waiting for the children's presence before unleashing their flood. Lightning and resounding claps of thunder provided a suitable backdrop as the evil that resided within these bald-faced boys shown for the first time, within a few short hours of their crossing into the town's borders.

At the time of their arrival, Bishop could be found slowly forging his way to the recyclery, long twisted double-braided rope pulled tight over his shoulder, hundreds of pounds worth of scrap metal in tow, eyes closed to the world, his path all-too-familiar to his feet. As the first few drops of water fell to the ground, Bishop stopped walking, eyes slowly opening to the earth, the dark wet spots mudded up onto the bone-dry dirt road he was trudging. Bishop gazed briefly to the skies as a drop of rain fell onto his cheek, carving a muddy path as it trickled down to his beard. With this, Bishop closed his eyes and continued his journey.

As the storm began, Tribe was exiting the doors of the recycling plant, having received his due for a load of copper he had brought in, never mind where it came from. Looking westward toward the billowing gray clouds, Tribe could piece together Bishop's figure in the distance, moving slowly towards the facility. With that, Tribe rode off, heading God knows where, but certain to return.

There they stood, the gang of boys, on the edge of town, scanning, plotting, unwelcome by a place that for a few final moments, had no idea they existed at all.

Being men of inaction, Bishop and Tribe may never have stood up to these newcomers had they decided to make money by some other means than stealing and selling car batteries to the local recyclery. Cruel and unusual is a phrase that once had been used to describe the acts these boys carried out indiscriminately on both locals and passersby. It is a travesty for this town, that that phrase would be cut down to just 'cruel', as the insidious behavior became less and less unusual and much more commonplace.

It had been maybe two weeks before the boys decided they needed to find a means to make money. Up to this point they had stolen whatever they needed, becoming more brazen in the crimes they committed. The boys had their eyes now fixated on something they could not steal, and therefore needed to find cash. Any filling station or market was aware enough of their existence and had full intentions to alarm the sheriff if any of the 3 had shown their faces around their parts. So, in the dark cover of night, the gang would steal the batteries from whatever vehicles they could find and race them to the recycling plant the next day.

Things went on like this for a number of weeks, maybe even a month or two. After these weeks or months had worn down on the people of this town, and on the wallets and well-being of both Bishop and Tribe, it had become more than obvious that the supposed law of the town had no intention or ability to bring the hellish gang of children to justice.

I wish I could say that Bishop and Tribe had formed some sort of alliance and set out to end the evil ways of the boys. Truth be told, it was the kids came looking for the men. Shameful the way those children went at Bishop, beating him and such, until there was no visible inch of his flesh that weren't covered in blood. They let him live that time, the plan was to let him sore up, start to heal, then come back to give him another round.

Used to be that if someone was on the wrong side of ya, you just shot him. With these young devils there would be no quick ending and no remorse could be found in em at all; not one ounce. It wasn't much after they left Bishop that they found Tribe. The young and well-trained Tribe was waiting for them, already figuring that any day they would be after him.

As the gang busted through the front door of Tribe's meager apartment, Tribe came out from his corner, quickly laying waste to the otherwise formidable Georgie. I imagine the last sounds Georgie heard would be that of his neck being twisted in all sorts of unnatural directions.

With the swift death of Georgie the two remaining boys scattered and fled the premises, beating the pavement toward anywhere that wasn't near Tribe. Tribe gave chase and followed the effeminate Hue to a scrap yard near the recyclery. Having lost Hue somewhere in the maze that made up the yard, Tribe scrambled to find the source of a gunshot. The source had been a bloody but now ambulatory Bishop, standing over the dead brother of the gang's leader. Fitting as it was to see Hue meet his end at the scrap yard, something didn't seem right about big brother Malice not being there to see his kin close his eyes that final time, though he certainly would not be too far away from the scuffle.

Tribe approached Bishop steadily, the body about 20 feet between the two of them as the next sound, the psychotic ravings of Malice, came from behind a compactor. However close Malice had previously been to that proverbial edge of sanity, seeing his brother laying there in his own blood had pushed him well over. Metal on metal clanked loudly as Malice moved around the compactor, pounding the butt of his gun on the machine. Quiet ravings quickly turned to screams as the madness flowed like tears out of the boy. As the men trained their sights on the kid, each raised their arms toward one another.

There they were, Bishop, Tribe, and Malice, frozen in a three-man standoff, each hand clutching a gun, locked and aimed. A nearly incapacitated Bishop would undoubtedly be the slowest trigger to pull, all present stood there knowing he was at a complete disadvantage. The tensions were sharpest between Tribe and Malice. Tribe aimed with a cool hand directly between the eyes of his opponent, and Malice twitchingly aimed in return, synapses in his twisted brain trying to figure out which of the two men he would kill first, the old and slow, or the young and unflinching. Indeed he could fell Bishop, hope to survive the skirmish with Tribe and then split the territories between the two instead of the lot; and if he succeeded in killing Tribe, he could kill off Bishop at his leisure.

As his finger began to squeeze the trigger at Bishop, a thunderous bang echoed off the steel compactor from behind Malice, Tribe got off the first shot, and that was the only one needed. The bullet came out of Malice's head just as quickly as it had entered, patterns of red and gray mixed on the side of the trash compactor he stood in front of; his body now as limp and lifeless as his cohort's.

As the boom from the gun continued to echo its way through the skies, silence filled the spaces between the two remaining men, each with one gun still aimed at the other. With a grateful sigh, Tribe lowered his piece to the ground, happy that he did not have to take another life today, unhappy that he had returned to that way of life at all. Bishop stared at the man 30 years his junior from behind the sight of his gun as Tribe smiled and said one word:

"Coffee?"

Tribe's invitation had been the first bit of warmth Bishop would have felt since the young man and his mother left town all those years ago.

When Bishop pulled that trigger he did so with regret.

The Morning of the Early Sun

A man ran for cover under the canopy of a bus stop one rainy afternoon. Before the rain, the man simply wondered the streets, feeling as though the concrete maze had beckoned to him from his small, dank apartment. The man sat under the canopy on a bench, hunched forward with elbows resting on the tops of his knees. As he recovered his breath, his gaze fell from the horizon of endless skyscrapers to the canvass of curbs, potholes and drainage apertures. The man watched as the gathering waters rushed through the streets and fled away to the ditches and the drains, carrying with it refuse from the cigarette-laden cityscape. The man's eyes watched the caravan of discarded smokes, wondering if they had belonged to anyone he had known or once cared for, and in the mix of those moments the man had spotted something stuck in the waste.

The man watched the item, square and beige as it remained lodged to the curb in spite of the rushing deluge. He felt it call to him; summon him in a similar fashion as the streets had. 'Perhaps,' he thought, 'this is what I set out to find. Perhaps this is what I was sent to see.' The man came out from under the awning and watched as taxis, cars, vans, and all matter of urban transport rushed by. He waited for his moment to jet across the street and salvage his mystery item. Again out of breath from the adventures of street-crossing, the man bent down, plunged his hand into the advancing waters and gripped what he soon discovered to be a book.

Staring down at his find, the noise of the busy downtown melted away and the only sounds that remained were the pattering of raindrops falling on the waterlogged book cover. In this way, the same way in which he felt compelled to venture out from his small and dank apartment, break from the rain under a bus stop, risk death by traffic, the man could feel his book speaking to him, as it if had purposefully been waiting in a shallow pool of waste for these moments and surely the ones to follow. The world returned to the man as he tucked the book under his arm and beneath his coat and began his return home.

The man shook off the rain and whatever cold air had followed in from the hallway outside of his apartment. He dropped his long coat to the floor and grasped his find with both hands, examining the cover for any discernible markings, titles, names. The book itself was plain and otherwise unremarkable, but the mystery that surrounded its unearthing puzzled and excited the man to no end. The man twisted the knob on his oven to the lowest setting before inserting a leaf of paper towel between each page of the book. The man watched through the oven door, praying silently that the oven and paper towels would dry the book without igniting anything. Blinking only when absolutely necessary, the man spent hours in front of that oven, watching as the heat dried the pages and the pools of water slowly evaporated from the cover.

That day turned into evening and night quickly crept into the apartment as the man withdrew the book from his oven. A small smile broke through his lips as he opened the book and his eyes were able to distinguish letters and words and punctuation. The same 26 letters he was familiar with had taken on a new meaning to the man for no other reason than their arrangement on those pages.

A simple story, 56 small pages from cover to cover, the man's fingers and eyes caressed the pages as he filled his mind with this new and brief world. This was a story of Gabe, a man who was, on the whole not unlike the man who found the book that day.

...Gabe found himself sitting up in bed, realizing now that it had been months since his last good night of sleep. His arms behind him, Gabe propped himself up, sheets draping around his waist and hair falling around his eyes. His head hung, chin resting on his chest as the thunder rumbled through the night. An hour and a half had passed with Gabe sitting there in his bed. Something outside of his window caught his eye as his head tilted toward whatever it was. Without enough time to form a thought, the Sun burst through the clouds, arriving a few hours early on this particular day. The sun cut through the clouds, the rain ceased and even the thunder was afraid to rumble under the brilliance of the new light. Gabe's eyes squinted and his hand raised to block out the radiance, but it bled around his hand and continued to invade his eyes.

Gabe had been a man that sought only validation of the idea that he existed at all. Throughout his life his family had taught him the merits of distrust. Gabe, through meticulous design had found a way to exist without his name on a single bill, courtesy of an acquaintance that had gone over seas and needed an apartment sitter. Gabe had a phone that didn't require a name and had just as many in its list of contacts. He had no job but, again through meticulous planning and execution, did have a nice roll of cash stuffed into a pair of pants that gravity had folded on the floor of the bedroom.

That morning, the morning of the early Sun, Gabe threw on his clothes and lumbered down a few flights to the lobby of the apartment building to check his acquaintance's mail. Gabe closed the window to the mail slot, opting to wait for it to fill with more envelopes before taking it back upstairs. Gabe was still filled with the daylight that broke through his window that morning, though none of it shown. Gabe left the apartment building and began his way down the street to some place uncertain, stomach grumbling with hunger. Rain water from the night had gathered in a puddle that overran the curbside about a block from where Gabe was heading. He continued on his path, looking one moment to the next block, waiting to avoid the water that had built up, and then glancing back down at the ground, watching the tips of his shoes as they marched quietly toward that uncertainty. Gabe glanced up to see a woman waiting on a bench, feet raised off the ground, avoiding that puddle that had overtaken the curb. Gabe had not noticed her sitting there before, but her figure was undeniably there now. Her bus approached and she searched unsuccessfully for a dry spot to stand on. Gabe watched as she closed her eyes tightly and lowered her feet to the water and began to stand. As her eyes closed Gabe began to notice her beauty. In that realization he would have believed that she would have been graceful enough to simply stand on that pool of water and not get a single drop on her. Such was not the case in this reality, and the water surrounded her feet. Nearly as quickly as she stood she had begun to fall. Gabe rushed and grabbed at her shoulders, stopping her fall. The woman looked down to find her footing and avoid the embarrassment of making eye contact with whomever had saved her from falling completely. As she returned to her feet, eyes down, Gabe lowered his head to meet her eyes. With this gesture she lifted her head and her eyes shown into Gabe's with the same intensity and splendor as the early sun that morning. His pupils became tiny as her light filled him, and even his stomach was afraid to rumble in the brilliance of her eyes.

Stunned by her light, Gabe stumbled backwards. She began to step forward, as if to catch him in the same way that he had caught her. Gabe recovered unassisted and stared at her for a moment that seemed to continue on for hours. She smiled in a very nervous and equally charming way as her face turned down as if to hide from his stare.

'I'm Eileen.' Were the only words she needed to speak. A silence hung in the air before Gabe realized that she was being pleasant to him.

"I...I'm Gabe." he responded, a very nervous and equally charming grin spreading over his face, the first of his light to shine in years.

Eileen had forgotten about her bus, a fact that had made the bus driver grow impatient. Like a hog, the driver grunted, "c'mon if your comin' on."

Eileen turned around without moving her feet, and with an urgency in both expression and action, she waved the bus on. The door to the bus closed and the vehicle pulled away.

"I'm heading to a diner for lunch." Eileen stated, hoping Gabe would understand that to be an invitation.

Gabe watched her speak in awe. For a moment, Gabe had felt fear that in speaking, in moving at all, her light may be expended much in the way he believed his to have been. What Gabe didn't know was that his light had begun to shine as well and that his glow radiated from him in a way that Eileen had never experienced. His mouth agape, she chuckled nervously and said "Maybe you could come with me? Up on 56th?"

"Sonny's?"

"Yeah...that's the one."

The man continued to read the story of how Gabe came to know Eileen. The two fell in love quickly and shared their light with each other. Through his time with Eileen, Gabe was able to find the light in himself which he once believed to be lost for good. The man found himself unable to put the story down or even look away. Page after page he read waiting for the inevitable 'bad news' or struggle to come to the pair. Page after page he read, watching these two fall in love and change each other's lives in deep and profound ways.

Confused by his captivation, the man eventually began to understand that this particular love story was empty of any turmoil. There were no deep dark secrets, no last minute cancers to fight or car wrecks or muggings to contend with or push through. The man who found the book began to understand inside of himself that this world had taught him the merits of distrust, just as Gabe's upbringing had. The man began to see that the things we find right in front of us, such as a rain-washed book could impact us in profound and meaningful ways, much as Gabe and Eileen had. He started to understand that the light inside of him, his own beauty and worth, as with Gabe, were stifled only by his belief that it didn't exist at all.

The book ended abruptly, Gabe and Eileen continuing on together as they always had. There had been no indication that they ended up happily ever after, or if they ended at all. For all the man knew, this pair could still be out there, if they existed in the first place. The man closed the book and set it on his lap, playing through everything he knew from the story, searching for an ending in his mind but unable to decide how he believed the story would go if he had written it.

The man spent the rest of the day pacing around his apartment; captivation followed him around his home like a hungry puppy. He would look out the window from time to time, noticing only the passing of the day. Night fell upon him and he found his way to bed.

The next day the man woke from his bed rejuvenated and well rested. He made his breakfast and went about his usual morning routine. He felt again called to venture out to the busy streets of the city.

He descended the stairs of his apartment building and stopped to check his mail. His attentions initially broken by a man whispering to himself and avoiding eye contact with all who may have heard him. As he reached his hand toward the envelopes in his box, the man smiled as the thought of Gabe leaving the envelopes to pile up entered his mind. The man, still smiling, began to close his mailbox as a young woman he was not familiar with began checking her mail just a few boxes over. He had noticed her for a brief moment before she turned to him, nervously introducing herself.

"Hi, I'm new to the building, I'm Rose."

The man paused as he looked her in the eyes, her pupils grew tiny and he said to her:

"Hi, I'm Gabe."

An Imperfect Fortress

"Tell me the first thing you remember then."

"From when?"

There I sat, in the doctor's office, the Shrink's office, surrounded by the reality that I would eventually have to tell this man things I never wanted to talk about.

"From the accident? You already know all about what happened."

"Not the event, son...after. Tell me what you remember following the event."

I hated it when he called me 'son.' It sounded too deliberate and empty of anything resembling genuine feeling or concern.

I sat there for a moment, diving into my mind, passing by as many of the painful and emotionally nerve-raping parts as I could...again surrounded by a quickly enclosing reality of discomfort.

"Well Doc," my "Doc" intentionally left as empty as his "son" had been, "I remember...dreaming."

"Dreaming?"

"Yes...dreaming about a memory."

"Tell me about that."

"The memory was from when we were younger, maybe our freshman year of high school. It was me and Max."

"Melody's brother."

"Yes, M..Melody's brother. He developed physically a year or so before the other boys in our class. I always assumed it was because he and Melody were twins..."

"-And since girls typically hit puberty before boys...his started when hers did."

I tapped my finger to the tip of my nose to indicate to the doc that he had figured out my logic...some sarcasm was involved.

"By the time we were starting high school, Max could more or less grow the beginnings of a beard inside of a week or so. There was one evening over at his house, he told me that his body hair was starting to make him self-conscious and that he had heard most girls don't like boys with lots of body hair. I smiled and told him not to worry. He asked why and I told him that back in the 80's, some of the most sought-after men in Hollywood were furry. Ya know, Tom Selleck, Robin Williams...guys like that. He didn't immediately take me at my point.

I could see in his eyes that my words hadn't helped, so I told him "everything comes back…it's just a matter of time.'""

"Heh." the doc let out a small laugh. "And?"

I looked up at him, my eyes had settled downward and to the side during the course of my story.

"And then I heard the beeps."

"The beeps?"

"Yeah doc, the beeps."

We had been friends for as long as I can remember, the three of us. We met as children, played as children do, grew as children do. We experienced life together, each bringing our unique views to the group. We lived, we changed. We changed, but we never left each other.

My family moved when I was 4 years old or so to the house I would grow up in and the house that my folks still call home. My parents would later explain to me that they were wanting to start trying for another child. They so loved being parents that they wanted to give me a little brother or sister, a desire that never came to be. My father's best friend, colleague and business partner Dr. Emmett Black had told my dad about a beautiful house next door to his that just hit the market and would be more than large enough to accommodate a growing family.

I don't remember much of the move because of my young age, but to hear the story told by father, I was about as excited as a 4 year old could get. He had promised me a big surprise once we arrived at the new place, and from the moment those words left his mouth I wouldn't shut up about it.

We trekked from one end of town, the end of town without surprises, and headed toward our new home. When we left our old house, I didn't spend too much time saying good-bye. I didn't focus on the things I was leaving, instead I fixated myself on this mystery that would be awaiting me at our new place…as much as a 4 year old could I suppose.

Every stop light and every stop sign would bring about a new and eager protest from my shrill 4 year old voice. We had turned on to our street and made our way down a few blocks, my cries coming out as we passed every second or third house, "Is that it?! Is that it!?" not caring whether or not there were already children playing in the driveways or otherwise laying claim to the homes we passed.

By the time we pulled into our new driveway my head had all but detached from my body as it searched and scanned at all angles for anything that looked remotely as though it would be meant for me. The door to the old Dodge Caravan slid open and as soon as I could I was out of the vehicle and searching like a bloodhound for what I eventually discovered waiting for me behind the wrought-iron fence that separated the front yard from the back: my playground.

Sensing trepidation in lieu of excitement, my father picked me up and sat me on his shoulder. In knowing that he was there, staring this thing down with me, knowing there was no need to be afraid, any hesitation left me.

I learned many years later that my father had been beside himself with excitement for several days to show me the playground that came with house. From his shoulder, so many feet up in the air, I could see it all; the slides and the swings and the knotted climbing ropes. I squirmed with the same excitement my father must have been feeling in the days leading up to that moment. He correctly interpreted that as a sign to let me down, and as my sandal-led feet hit the ground I took off toward the play-scape.

It wasn't too long after I had begun tirelessly trying to scale the mountain of obstacles that I heard my mother calling to me. Looking over to her, I caught my first glimpse of Melody, her twin brother Max, and their father Dr. Black.

As children, Max and Melody were cute, curly-haired tornadoes with round bellies, bright blue eyes and easily excitable, curious personalities. They were everything I wasn't. Again, to have my father tell the story, you would by comparison to the twins, think that I was some social retard of a 4 year old. Max and Melody had never met someone they didn't feel comfortable being held by, a fact which often got them into trouble. I, on the other hand had grown to be the wary, cautious type, content only in the arms of my parents.

My mother introduced me first to the doctor as I stole glances and cowered behind her legs. Dr. Black crouched down from his six-foot-four frame, smiled and waved to me. Still crouching, he turned and signaled for his two children to join him. They had both been in the yard playing with my father, a bit more extraverted to him than I had been to theirs. I watched the family gather from the gate; still completely hidden behind my mother's legs, unsure of what to think of my new best friends.

Without difficulty my mother gathered me into her arms and introduced me to the doctor, now joined by his wife. As the children, just a few months younger than me, bounded toward us, my father followed and took us all to my new playground in the hopes that I would come out of my shell if for no other reason than to show off my slide-and-swing-covered monolith.

By the end of that night, and the end of many, many nights following that one, our parents had to all but tear us away from each other. That's where it all started, with the forming of a life-long friendship between the three of us: Max, Melody and Sam. It's difficult to imagine that was 20-plus years ago but it was.

Our identities developed in the context of the group. Each of us reacting to our surroundings and watching to see how the other would behave. Max would tell you that every bad idea he ever had or every ill-fated misstep he had taken were the result of my mind's twisted ambitions. He would tell you that I would play for hours and then retreat for hours, even if I never left his side.

If you were to ask Melody, she would tell you that I could make her laugh harder than anyone else, but that she knew I only did that because hearing her laugh brought such enormous pleasure to me. She would tell you that for a time she found me to be very creepy, choosing to sit out of an occasional game so that I could watch her and her brother play. Melody would tell you that I was the one who initiated our relationship, and that I was infatuated with her long before she even noticed I was a boy; she would be half right at least.

This story is an attempt to complete a long and painful process that I started some time ago. This story is my last best effort to alleviate a tremendous burden of guilt that has been on my shoulders for far too long. While I know that I can never fully rid myself of it, it is my sincerest hope that in sharing this story, I can at the very least find some sort of attrition for the things that I have done. Everyone carries with them the knowledge of consequence. That knowledge for me comes from not being able to let go, knowledge gained from losing not only the person I had loved more than anything else, but from not allowing myself to accept an end.

Beeps. It had been the beeps that woke me. I remember thinking that it was an alarm clock going off. I wanted to move. I wanted to move my arm and I wanted to shut off the beeping. God my arms were so heavy, I couldn't move. It was after the fourth or fifth rhythmic passing that I understood from where the beeps had come. I could feel my heart begin to hasten, I could hear the beeps follow suit. My eyes opened slowly, adjusting to the mid-day sun shining through the window. I woke up in a hospital room.

Standing near the window were my parents, aesthetically drained from a night of panic and miles of pacing. I remember that moment and the ones that followed even more vividly than the ones from the previous night. I remember the blackness that receded as my eyelids opened. The sun poured in from behind my mother, casting a shadow as thin as her frame and illuminating it just the same. I remember breathing in and turning my attention to my father, standing to Mom's side, woefully looking down at his son. I remember being flooded with thoughts but not being able to articulate a single one of them. God, I remember at that next moment knowing that she was gone. I remember feeling empty. Feeling shaken. I remember looking at the bed I was in, seeing my body lying under the sheets. I remember thinking it was odd that I wasn't in a hospital gown and that with the exception of my shoes, I had been left fully clothed, but then again I wasn't sick. I remember following that thought with vomit. Dad walked to the hallway and asked for someone, and I kept throwing up, knowing it wouldn't stop, and for a long while, it didn't. I threw up until there was nothing left to expel. It continued until my sides cramped and ached and I could feel my pulse throbbing in my neck and temples, and then I heaved more. The pressure in my head grew from the heaving to the point that I could see a singular dark spot through my eyes, as if someone were pushing on them from the sides. I don't know how long it went on, but when it stopped I felt worse than I ever had, the taste of bile and acid on my tongue, the fumes burning in my throat. The end result was a very weak and pitiful me sobbing and curled up; grasping at my pillow and my shirt. That is everything I remember until waking up again.

By late afternoon I had been roused, now re-hydrated thanks to a series of liquid-filled, clear, medical-grade plastic bags. I fought with myself, I fought with my feelings, my memories of what had happened the previous night, it was…fuzzy.

I could see and remember clear as day how the evening started. Melody and I went to eat at that Italian restaurant, then we were going to play cards at her parent's house to celebrate our engagement. As I was telling all of this to my folks and the doctor's in the room, I gathered that we had never made it home after the party.

My mother came and sat beside me on the hospital bed, a clear trail of tears cut through her make-up covered cheeks. Panic set in again as I began to ask about Melody. No one would give me anything remotely resembling a straight answer.

I demanded to know where she was, how she was, why she wasn't there with me. Pleading now through my own tears, I started groping at the I.V.'s in my arm in a sort of anguished protest meant to signify my intent on leaving to find my fiancé. As the commotion began to pick up, we were interrupted by a nurse whose only words were "she's out now."

We had all been introduced; the kids that is, the adults were all very familiar with each other. We had all been expected to get along and play as kids should…to be friends…and the three of us, Max, Melody and I had no problems living up to that demand. Between the two families' homes there was no shortage of square footage or places to play. My giant playground in the backyard minuscule when compared to the size of our home. There was nothing to this new home that I wasn't in love with. Our main floor was a beautiful maze of rooms that flowed wonderfully from one to the next. My room was located down the hallway at the top of the stairs; stairs originating from the kitchen, as if designed for an ever-hungry-and-growing teenage boy. I had my own bathroom, and a decently large bedroom that I eventually decorated myself. I had a south-facing view with a window that gave me a wonderful view into Max and Melody's room. As children with walkie-talkies we would stay up into the late hours of the weekends, chatting with each other in static-laden sentences. Ppssshhh…over and out.

Max eventually moved out of that room, and after some other developments that window of mine became a very interesting, provocative and educational lens into Melody's room.

Getting to where we are now, I look back to the time right before the disaster…and it's so bittersweet, as I imagine it would be for you and any of your childhood memories. I remember things, some of course more vividly than others, as I imagine it would be for you and any of your childhood memories. The bittersweet comes from remembering how it all felt as a child, how innocent life was, going through that loss of innocence, knowing that your life was changing and you were growing from your acts, from your decisions. Between the days of that first summer, and the final days of my senior year of high school, Max, Melody and I grew, as kids do, and became very close, as friends do. I wish that I could say all of my memories are good ones, hell I would even settle for accurate, but they are mine and I guess that is enough. We have pictures, quite a few really if you put the collection of the two families together. We have a few scars, Max's are the worst but we survived all of it together. I have so many of these memories…ones that I can draw on and try to describe, but I feel like even the timid and adolescent scribbling of a kid with a fresh memory and a box of crayons can be better than that of a full-grown adult trying to recall these sorts of things. I know that I can sit here and tell you about the time the three of us were jumping on a trampoline that belonged to a woman a few houses down. I can tell you we weren't supposed to be down there, and we were definitely not supposed to be on that trampoline. I could tell you how scary it was, every jump, watching Max eventually succeed in bouncing Melody through the air only to land on the ground with one arm mangled in the springs.

I could try to tell you how acrid the blood smelled, and how warm it was. I could try to tell you how loud she yelled and how shrill her crying was. I could tell you that we were about 10 years old, and none of us had ever been so scared.

Now, I know that if I had been writing all of this on the day it happened, I could tell you, even in as basic of words as I have already, but with more sincerity and fear and credibility the events of that day, and all because it was fresh, because 'the blood would still be wet,' as it were.

Max and I had started our short journey down the long path of friendship that day on my playground. It seemed within the first few years that the two of us would already have an entire life's worth of memories together; at each other's side through the easiest and toughest days of childhood, adolescence, early adulthood. In fact I don't believe our loyalty to one another had been tested until my relationship with his sister intensified. Best friend status notwithstanding, no one really smiles when they find out you've slept with their sister.

Max and I had been in nearly every class since our first day of school so many years ago. The process of friend-making never really appealed to me as a kid. Max on the other hand was as sweet and per-sonable as anyone I imagine there is. Even from such a young age, he had been charming and charismatic; everything he needed to be to en-sure someone would be excited or at least willing to participate in his endeavors. His looks developed at a pace that rivaled Melody's, whose figure began to fill out in the early stages of 5th grade. By that reckon-ing Max's body was nearly two full years ahead of the other boy's in our grade. For the record my changes started somewhere between the two.

Before puberty found Max, he had been one of the smaller boys in school; his sister even surpassed his height for a brief moment in time. Max's early development at one point became a sore topic, as he had been ridiculed by one of the boys in our class. This much smaller boy had by poked fun at Max at the start of 6th grade for having undergone damn near every change he was going to go through. Max was taller than most kids at that point and smelled terribly on hot days and even had the beginnings of a mustache if his face had not been properly tended to over three or four days. As mentioned, we were middle-schoolers, but Max was already bench pressing at a high school level.

For one reason or another this boy thought that he would demon-strate his idiocy by picking a fight with the much larger Max. Max had been determined to make friends with the kid but after one punch to his nose, Max dropped those aspirations as quickly as he had dropped the other kid to the floor. I stepped in to make sure no more punches would be thrown, and though we had been lifelong friends, that was the day Max and I saw each other as brothers. Max hated himself for giving in to that other boy's remarks and for knocking him down as he had. He thanked me for standing up to him on behalf of the other kid; a view I hadn't previously shared. My intention had simply been to stop Max before he wound up in even more trouble. In trying to stop Max for Max's own sake, but he saw me step in to prevent him from falling even deeper into his own darker, more aggressive side. Max eventually allowed himself to drop the guilt after apologizing to the boy and even standing up for him later on in high school, when it became obvious that the boy would never be able to stand up to some of the higher level bullies.

In spite of the fact (or perhaps because of it) that he was so physi-cally developed over the rest of us, Max decided to dedicate a big portion of his spare time to building his physique. Because of his size, right from the first few years of high school, Max had become a very sought-after item at the top of any coach's list, and something of a la-dies man. Though Max became a rather imposing figure, cut out for the more aggressive sports he preferred to be found on the stage. I always blamed it on his one and only fight with the boy in middle school, but Max used his charm instead of his muscles to diffuse every tight spot he found himself in, and there were plenty. He ensured his popularity with his personality, and he guaranteed his safety with his physique. Max was the unofficial guardian and protector of the weak at our school and everyone knew that to be fact. The smaller kids looked up to him for it and the girls flocked to him for it. Max had been voted the 'school's friendliest' in the yearbook our senior year. His kind nature had taken root deeply in his personality and its only competition was the playfulness and audacity that had always been part of Max's DNA.

Melody however, went the other direction because of her early physical maturing. Where Max came out of his shell from the attention his developing had garnered, Melody became shy and meek from stares young boys would give her, even if at that age they weren't yet sure as to why. Once playful as a child, she withdrew further into her blossoming body from the perverse behavior she began to notice from the less-fair of the sexes. There had, throughout her first months as a young woman, even been a man, our bus driver, who had made several perverse comments to Melody about her budding shape. This man is never talked about by the family, and while I am sure Dr. Black would rather me not mention it at all, it is a credit to her father that, at his urging, the city police took a closer look at the bus driver, a man who is no longer in a position that he can hurt any child.

Throughout our days in middle school, my relationship with Melody remained as it always had, that is to say, she was one of my best friends. The identical smile she shared with her brother was one that I often took on as my own, 'the third twin' as their mother used to refer to me. As mentioned earlier, my folks had always wanted another child, and while they never conceived again, they treated the twins as though they had been born into our home from the beginning.

Melody eventually tired of Max and mine's antics and pranks, maybe that arm-mangling from the trampoline had something to do with it, maybe it didn't, but whenever Max and I would return to either house after an evening of mischief, Melody would be there with popcorn waiting to be popped and a movie to be watched. That became our dynamic for a long time, several years in fact. We three would gather and watch movies in someone's basement. We would laugh at the comedies Max would pick, hoping to find some inspiration as to his next hijinks; we would cower under the cover of a shared blanket on the couch when we felt brave enough to sneak a scary movie past our parents, and we would sit uncomfortably in separate chairs whenever Melody would force a romantic girly-flick on us.

High school came for Melody the same as it had for me and Max. Max discovered drama club, I had my own interests, and Melody found herself in books and obsessed with classic pop music. If ever Max had stayed hours after school let out for theater, I would walk home with Melody, or if I missed her, I could find her holed up in her room, reading whatever caught her fancy and listening to Men At Work.

Sure there would be times that either Max or Melody or both would come to find me; it's not like I was the obnoxious neighbor kid that always invited himself over or never got the hint that his 'friends' weren't that into him. I guess I just hadn't by that point, found anything to identify myself with in the ways that Max or Melody had. I had them, and I had my alone time and time with my folks.

I suppose, if I had to pick any point in time that I had been happiest, this would be second only to the years that followed. Middle school and the first two years of high school had been so much fun for so many reasons; I had Max and Melody, they had me and each other, and with the exception of homework, we had very little responsibility and were allowed to be kids. I miss those times so very much, and, again, if forced, would say that the only time greater than this period of my life would be the one that came next.

Melody and I had fallen for each other long before either of us had realized it. I couldn't tell you when our time together became dates instead of simple time spent. But I do remember the night I began to see her through new eyes. Eyes that saw her as beautiful and sexy and still familiar, as if I had always known her in this new way. I remember the revelation of her.

Every year for a couple of weeks in June Max and Melody would be shipped off to a summer camp. This was a camp for twins (who knew such things existed at all) so I wasn't allowed to go, and thus found myself overly lonely and often times wishing I had more than just two friends in this world.

One summer evening my ever-intuitive father had picked-up on my boredom and invited me to pizza and a movie to help keep me occupied on a very rainy day in the middle of the two-week friend-drought. We went to our favorite pizza place in the early afternoon and planned on having plenty of time to catch the 2:40 show. How funny that so many details stick out in my mind about this day, the time of the show (though I have no idea what movie we went to), the cheap jokes my father was throwing my way in the hopes of garnering a smile (how can you identify a dogwood tree), and how the smell of a warm summer rain could overpower the heavy odor of grease and red sauce whenever the door would open (by its bark).

My memory is a trait that must've been given to me from my mother. About half-way through his second slice my father realized that he "remembered to forget his box of candy" to sneak into the theater. We wolfed down the last few bites and cleansed our pallets with soda and haste, making our way to the door, to the car, to home. Dad ran in to get his candy, I to retrieve a newer, dryer, hoodie. Peeling off my rain-saturated shirt and flinging open the door to my closet my eyes caught a much more interesting and curious view from the Black household. Melody was in her room. She must have seen the movement in my room; by the time my eyes found her she was already smiling and waving. Within a few brief moments she had left her room and my phone was ringing.

Melody had a new excitement in her voice. It was new to me at least; something fresh and playful. I miss her voice as much as I miss anything else. She had called to ask me to come over and hang out. I had asked her why she was home instead of at camp, a question she dodged. I told her about my afternoon movie plans with my dad so we settled on a movie night of our own later that evening at her place. I remember hanging up the phone and my dad questioning the grin on my face; he was upset because my phone call had put us even more behind schedule than the candy run. As we sat through the movie I could only think of Melody's final words to me over the phone that day: 'I can't wait.'

"She's out. What does that mean 'she's out?' Was all that could come through my confusion and fear.

Looking back at my mother, nestled again under my father's arm, I could see the cold vein of fear coursing through her tired posture. Looks turned to glances which turned to nervous surveys of expressionless faces as I began to piece together the events of the previous night.

Like a torrent unleashed from a broken dam I was drowned in the memories of those moments. In a pitiful and sedated attempt I attempted to stand, demanding to be taken to Melody, my tone now void of pleading and question.

"Son." My father's only word to me in that room. I turned to him, his resolve easily discernible and equal to my own. I was frozen, so eager to leave and find what they had done to Melody, but needing badly to acknowledge the pain and fear that had replaced the hope and love that resided in me a short number of hours ago. I continued out of the room, honestly not knowing at all which way to go, which hall to go down. I became that hospital for those moments, searching the inside of myself with the same frantic energy I had outwardly assumed. Floor by floor I searched, no one stopping or attempting to stop me, garnering only glances as I passed by each nurse station, one white-knuckled fist dragging my IV pole with me as I fought to keep myself from unraveling.

With every hallway new recollections of the previous night were delivered to my head with a throbbing blow. By the time I found her, found Melody, I had pieced together nearly every bit of that dreadful night and that horrific event. I looked through an observation window at her. Blood could be seen actively seeping through gauze and deliberately timed machine-regulated respiration could be heard as the doors next to the room opened and again closed. There was a highway of tubing inserted into her in so many places and with so many exits that I couldn't discern which fluids were going in and which were coming out.

I needed to hold her. One of the last things I remembered from the night before was that I had been screaming, crawling and trying desperately to get to her, to hold her as she lay there motionless on the grass. I put my hand on the glass of the observation window, surrounded now by silence and slow-moving people, feeling the pulse behind my eyes growing ever intense as my knees gave out. My father caught me as I fell, a pathetic and tear-soaked mess of a man sobbing and balled up on the floor. He stroked my hair as if I was a child, and I wished so badly to be that child again; either too young to understand what was happening or at least lied to in the hopes of delaying the inevitable revelation of mortality. It was there in that hallway that my stability first splintered, the seeds of my psychosis entered into my fractured mind, watered by my tears as I began to come undone.

My eyes burned as I looked over my father's shoulder to see Melody's parents approaching, they looked as though they had been in a war. Her mother angry and noticeably exhausted from the long wait of the surgery, her father frail, as though his facade of strength were about to collapse around him. I found a way to stand on shaky feet through the help of my dad, only to lose my stability as Dr. Black wraps his arms around me and said "It's ok, son," sentiments my father had not yet been able to articulate. My only response as I averted my gaze in shame, "It doesn't feel ok."

Melody's dad ducked his head to meet my eyes and as they locked, he somehow pulled me upright again.

"Sam," he said, "this wasn't you…this wasn't your fault."

We turned to look into the room through the glass. Melody, my love, his daughter, lay there motionless and vacant, still seeping from newly sutured wounds.

"Yes, it was."

"No," Dr. Black said, his voice filling with emptiness, "the other driver was on some drugs…he had no idea what he was doing, what he had done…he's fine." Those final words dripping with an ashamed anger.

My dad wrapped his arm around me and told me we had to go back to my hospital room, I needed to give some statements about the night before and they wanted me to talk to an on-site psychologist to "ascertain my mental state before releasing me."

We made our way back to the room, riding elevators in silence and trudged down hallways and around corners with a painfully slow gait, but it was all my legs could handle. Rounding our final turn by a nurse's station, my eyes lifted from the floor to see Max pacing by the doorway to my room.

That afternoon, between going to the movies with my dad and going over to Melody's house was one of the longest of my life, up to that point.

"I can't wait."

Those words resonated in my head for hours. I wish now that I had been able to respond before the phone clicked; maybe that would have helped to alleviate some of the anxiety coursing through me. I have no idea what I could have added, but surely something, anything would have helped.

After the movie ended and the credits began to roll (Planet of the Apes! Every few months our local theater would play a classic, that week was 'Planet') dad had asked if there was anything I wanted to do to kill time until dinner. I asked him if we had any microwave popcorn at home, a question that brought him confusion and eventual concern as we had both just consumed more than our fair share of salted and overly buttered popcorn.

To this day I am not wholly certain as to why I kept my plans for that night a secret from my folks. I had been over to Max and Melody's house a countless number of times before for movie nights. Maybe it was due in part to having just ventured to a movie with my dad and seeing another movie tonight would seem extraneous, or maybe it was because tonight, for the first time, it was no longer Max and Melody's house.

I spent the remainder of the time with my father answering the barrage of questions he had been firing at me in rapid succession; my one-word responses only adding to his concern. As we pulled into the driveway the tension inside of me grew in anticipation for the night, my evening with Melody still 4 hours away. I found my way up to my bedroom, completely bypassing my mother and her desire to find out how time with dad was.

Though the rain had stopped while I had been away at the movie theater, I stripped away my hoodie and shirt as I had earlier, strutting around my room in the hopes that Melody was still in her room looking on at my 150 lb. frame. After stealing a few subtle glances into her bedroom I accepted the simple reality that she wasn't there. I abandoned my nervous charade and, still naked from the waist up, decided on trying to relax and maybe even close my eyes to help pass the time.

It was that afternoon that I decided (after realizing that I was not at all capable of relaxing or turning off my mind) to make some changes to the setup of my room. That's a lie, I made one change. Using a couple of wooden storage frames my father had built a few years back in his 'hobby shed,' I elevated my bed to reach the lower seal of my very large window, the same window that the twins and I used to play in with our walkie-talkies as kids. Hiking up my bed had taken a good hour out of my afternoon, and soon after re-making my bed in the hopes that no one would realize the change, Mom called us all to dinner. It was still two hours before my time with Melody.

Time passed slowly at the table as my parents worked in tandem to drill me with questions about my reclusive behavior that day. Even if I had told them at this point that I was going next door they wouldn't have believed me. Going over to the Black household was such a common and innocuous happening that had I told them that they would have assumed that to be a ruse. I took that chance and finally came clean and tell them that Melody had come home early from camp and that I was going to go hang out there tonight and not to worry, I was fine. Not giving them the opportunity to respond I removed myself and my plate to retire yet again, to my room.

As the hour approached, I used my nervousness to prepare for the evening. I had begun to stink after the past few hours, sweat of anxiety mixed with the perspiration of repositioning my bed. A quick shower and re-application of deodorant, mixed with well-set hair and a sharp button-up and dark blue jeans and I would be all but set for the night. I had about 10 minutes left before heading over to Melody's and was about three buttons into putting on my shirt when I was overcome by a moment of curious clarity. It was undeniable now that I had felt so many varied feelings about that night but I hadn't for a single moment stopped to consider that Melody probably wasn't going through any of those anxious things herself. I realized in that moment that the tension and the nerves and anxiety I had allowed myself to store up that day were more than likely unfounded, and that now, bathed in a 50/50 cocktail of cologne and hair gel, I needed to quickly un-make myself.

I pulled off my nice clothes, grabbed a few loose-fitting rags to cover myself with, mussed up my hair, and even got in a few quick push-ups in the hopes that ANY man-stench would help cover the 'irresistible musky-oak' of my dad's cologne. I had dressed down about as much as I could while still remaining not repulsive and descended the stairs, oddly let down by the realization that Melody would not have seen tonight to be the date I had inexplicably hoped for. I grabbed a few bags of popcorn and went for the handle to the front-door and hollered that I would be next door should I be needed. I left the home followed only by a closing door and vapor trail of cologne fumes.

I approached the giant house next door with my usual stride and saw a fluttering in the living room curtains. As I approached I could hear only muffled shouts followed by the thudding of my heartbeat; my nerves had returned. An audible gulp followed hesitantly by a quick knock on the door and before I knew it, Mrs. Black had opened the door with a tremendous smile.

"She'll be right down Hun," she said, shutting the door with me still on the outside.

Moments later I was able to discern another round of quick shouts and Melody bounding down the stairs in the entry way. The door opened and there she stood, clad in her pajamas, out of breath, with her hair done up and specs of glitter still on her cheeks. I smiled nervously as she pulled me close for the first of a million hugs that would last longer than they should have, the flowery scent of her mother's perfume swirling in my nostrils from Melody's neck.

That night, the night I look back at and refer to as our 'first date' continued for a long while in awkward exchanges. My mind had been at least partially correct earlier that day, assuming that in fact the night would be just as any other, we would watch a movie, eat some popcorn and go about our ritualistic hang out as we had a million times before. I had, by that reasoning, been partially wrong as well, in some ways this night would be unlike any night before it. Though we knew the actions: make the popcorn, go downstairs, watch the movie, joke and be obnoxious, we stood in the kitchen trying desperately to come up with small talk.

"How was camp?"

"Meh, it was ok...missed it here."

Silence.

"What have you been up to since Max and I had left?"

"Nothing really, Dad has been on a bonding kick, so I've been with him a bunch."

Uninteresting silence interrupted by the DING of the microwave.

"What are we watching tonight?"

"What?"

"...The movie...which one did you get?"

And with her response I was as uncomfortable as I had ever been.

"It's called Swollen Romance."

Long. Terrible. Painful silence.

We went to the basement, I found my usual spot in the beanbag by the wall and Melody sat on the couch. We exchanged glances as the previews played through, a tradition at Max's insistence many years ago; watching the previews, not the glances.

The opening credits began as images of dried and dead leaves blew through an empty Manhattan street. A music-box theme ticked slowly by until the tune sweepingly progressed into a full orchestra of sound just in time for the title to fade in.

"Sure enough," I remember thinking, "I'm watching a movie called "Swollen Romance."

Melody looked at me and I at her, the ashamed smile on her face told me that she was excited for the next couple of hours and at the same time aware that I most likely was not. I remember turning down her offer of popcorn a few minutes into the movie for the chance to sit next to her. She accepted my terms and I found a spot by her. As the night went on, I found myself breaking the terms of the agreement to satisfy a salt craving, and though that meant putting up with the occasional flirtatiously stern expression, she never revoked my seating privilege. We watched the rest of the film under a shared blanket; my focus shifting between getting my heart to not pound so hard, and listening for hers. Though the noise of the movie filled the basement, I don't remember hearing a moment of it after moving next to Melody.

Sweet. Nervous. Excited silence.

The rest of the night went by and we found ourselves at her doorway. I told her I had a great time, the go-to line for any nervous boy trying to navigate the murky post-date waters. She read me like an open book and told me that she hopes to have more time with me soon...before Max comes home.

I looked at her and in a moment of terrified bravery I apologized:

"I'm sorry if this isn't what you were going for."

As she began to ask me what I meant, my lips met hers for the first time.

I kissed her.

I backed away, looking at her through uncertain and satisfied eyes.

She smiled a smile that I had never seen before. Before I could decipher its meaning her arms were around my neck and her kiss had overtaken my mouth.

Driving. Hopeful. Eager Silence.

After another of many embraces that would last longer than usual (and eventually tip Max off that we were seeing each other), Melody returned to under her doorway and said simply "Goodnight."

I could barely find the words to return to her. I waved with a stupor on my face and I walked home, replaying moments from that night in my mind, fighting to commit each one to long-term recall and praying to God that they did in fact happen.

I found my way to bed, unsure as to whether or not I was even tired. Most of my faculties had left me and been replaced with awe and excitement. I lay in bed, staring through my window; hoping to see the light in Melody's room flip on. I wished so badly to be a fly on the wall in whatever room she was in for no other reason than to see what expression she wore. She didn't return to her room that night. I found out months later that she had fallen asleep on the couch in the basement, huddled under the blanket that by then came to smell like my father and her mother, the blanket we had shared that night of our first date.

Melody and I knew that we had precious little time together before Max came home. It wasn't that we didn't want him to come home from the summer camp Melody had prematurely ditched, it's just that we were at a crossroads in our relationship. If things had become horribly awkward between us because of our kiss, then we knew we had to find a way to return to pre-kiss tendencies, and if things hadn't gotten weird...well then we needed to figure that out too.

To save you the suspense and me the embarrassment of re-living hormone-driven pubescent fumbling in dark rooms with my best friend's sister, I will say that our kiss lead us down a very fun path, and we decided to be together.

The camp was in late June/early July, so that was our first kiss. We took the three days following our first date to cover as many other firsts as we could so as to not find ourselves wrapped up in new experiences with Max in the room. We spent those days together walking around the local mall, flirting and laughing at the park, and then of course, there were those dark rooms I mentioned a moment ago. It's interesting when you fall for someone that you've known for so long and have already had so many experiences with. Even though I had been through that mall a countless number of times, or played at that park just as much, everything was different now...we were different now. I can't say that I remember all the old clichés about birds singing or colors being more vibrant but Melody, discovering her in this new way had been so amazing, everything we had done as friends I wanted to re-live for the first time with this new understanding of her.

Our three days had passed and Max returned from camp. Melody and I were both excited for him to come home; we just hadn't spent much time discussing how to approach the subject of 'us' when it came to him. I saw his car approach from the window in my bedroom and quickly made my way down the stairs and out the front door, heading straight to greet him. We hugged and I told him I had missed him, he called me a girl and then admitted to having missed me too. We both lit up as Melody came out of the house. Paying no attention to our synchronous "Hey!" to his sister, Max gave her a hug and made some comment razzing her for bailing camp early.

Melody brushed off his comment and came to stand next to me. We had been looking at each other when Max asked:

"So what did you guys do without me this week?"

Melody and I broke our gaze and looked to Max as though we had been children again, and our parents had just caught us trying to get the cookies down from the top of the refrigerator.

"Just...the usual" Melody was the first to get the words out.

"Yeah, movies and stuff like that." I added.

Max looked at me with bro-eyes.

"She make you watch a girly-flick?"

"My God yes!" I said with an exasperated tone.

Melody smacked my arm. The entire exchange was a ruse. While she did make me watch that awful movie, we both knew that I didn't mind it one bit, and neither did she. I knew in my heart at that moment as I am sure she did that keeping the curtain drawn on our relationship wouldn't be easy. Sure our folks would probably change the rules for movie nights and alone time for me and Melody if they knew about us, but lying to Max was a completely different game; one that I wasn't sure I would be able to play for long. When you go through big things in life, you go to your friends to talk about it and so on, and now I was going to be expected to refrain from that, and so was Melody.

We kept up the farce as long as we could, which ended up being all of about 3 weeks. We would hang out, the three of us just as we always had, but Melody and I had to start thinking up creative ways to find ourselves together. Max would suggest a movie night and Melody would offer to go pick up the movie, I would offer to go too and hope that Max wouldn't want to join us; Max ALWAYS wanted to join us. We had to sit in our usual spots in the basement. I would sit in my bean bag and try to count the number of times I looked over at Melody so that it didn't come across to Max that I was eyeballing his sister. And if it did, if Max called me on it, I had to come up with some lame excuse which more often than not involved embarrassing Melody just so Max would focus on laughing at her instead of thinking I was being creepy.

I knew it wasn't any easier for Melody, either. She would try to be discrete and avoid doing anything to draw attention to us, but any time her hand would graze mine or we found ourselves standing too close to each other, she would quickly pull her hand away or push me and laugh nervously. I'm sure in my head it was worse than in real life, but it's a small wonder that Max didn't pick up on things until the night he caught us. It was that night that everyone in both households found out and me and Melody, we have Max to thank for that.

The day before Max returned from camp, Melody and I had decided to dig out the old walkie-talkies from my attic. When my parents asked what we were doing digging around in the old boxes up there, we told them that we wanted to have the 'talkies ' out for when Max got home, so we could talk before bed like we used to. The truth was that we were never going to tell him at all, we just enjoyed having nighttime conversations over a line that our parents couldn't pick up on.

You'd have to ask Max, but if I remember correctly, and I like to think that I do, he busted the door down right after hearing his sister say through the bedroom door that she missed the feel of my hands under her shirt.

Between the two houses, Max was definitely the one who was least okay with me and Melody seeing each other. My folks were fine more or less, but tightened the rules when it came to our time spent together. Melody's folks were fine with it too, her father telling me that he knew that I was a good guy and had genuine feelings toward his daughter, and that I was close enough to reach should anything bad happen.

Max, in all of his rage, protested for the better part of the week. Once Melody and I were able to hold hands or kiss each other in front of Max, once we no longer had to hide or schedule lies, Max saw us for how happy we were together. He and I had a talk that pretty much involved me listening to him say he was happy that we were happy, but that he never wants to be put in the middle of any of our fights, and that he never wants to hear any of what he referred to as 'pleasure moans' during movie nights. Up to the day of the wreck Max would still make a fuss from time to time if he saw me kiss his sister, but he never riled us beyond childish levels.

Our relationship continued and developed over the next few months. School started back up; our senior year. Things were great with the three of us as a group, and Melody and I continued to fall for each other. We had taken things as far as we felt comfortable regarding the physical side of the relationship. I was beyond attracted to her, everything from the way she moved to the way she spoke was graceful and sexy. Fighting off certain feelings was difficult, always is I suppose when you're 17 and nearly everything gets you turned on or at the very least puts the idea of sex in your head.

We had the talk, deciding sex was going to wait. We didn't decide on when, just that it wouldn't be now. We also had the 'love' talk. I knew that I was in love with her, but I think she was torn when it came to committing to the words. We both felt the same for each other, and we had loved each other long before we ever said it, but deep down I think she was afraid that things could become fragile after admitting that to ourselves. Friendships like ours, or mine with Max, were incredibly durable and long-lasting and so far as our relationship was concerned, we were still before 'I love you's' and therefore able to go back to being just friends if needed. It wasn't until that New Year's Eve that it happened.

It was that night, New Year's night, the three of us had gathered in my room to watch the ceremonial ball drop and marvel at the amount of confetti and other refuse that would inevitably be left in the city streets of New York once everyone had cleared out. Myself and Melody sitting on my bed with our backs resting on the wall and Max relaxing in the neon-green beanbag that he brought from his basement, my old seat. Max would sneak looks over at his sister and I every few minutes to make sure that we were behaving. The ball dropped and we finished our snacks for the night. I walked the twins down to the front door; we all hugged, said congrats for some reason and promised each other we would hang out the next day.

I closed the door after watching my two friends begin the short trip across the yard and back to their home. I trudged quietly up the stairs and crawled into bed. I remember lying there on my back; thinking about how thankful I was for my friends and watching the sky as it slowly spit snow onto my window. I'm sure it wasn't long before I found my way to sleep. I'm not 100% sure, maybe an hour or so after I dozed off, I heard a light tapping on my door and raised my head to see my bedroom door inch open. It was Melody, she was dressed in her pajamas and was carrying a plastic grocery store sac in which she kept a wet item, which I later found out were her snow boots.

I remember letting out a sigh, surprised at just how scared I had been at the stirring in the middle-of-the-night. I sat up shirtless, wearing only a thin pair of pajama pants, hair mussed and fresh from my pillow. Melody smiled a familiar beautiful smile that could arouse me as much as it could sedate me and silently found her way to the edge of my bed. I remember looking at her and asking if everything was alright. You see the thing about Melody is that she was so secure and confident as any person I have ever met, but she would have these moments of need and charm that I do not anticipate ever being able to find in any other human being. She looked down at me, square in the eyes, placed her right hand gently on the left side of my face, fingers just under my ear, and hand running across my jaw-line. I dipped my head slightly to the left to rest in her hand; embracing it between my shoulder and face, in a loving and peaceful nudge. She leaned to me as if to tell me a secret.

"I love you."

I pulled my head back to look her in the eye. Her eyes were set and confident and loving and longing all at once.

"I love you, Mel."

She kissed me softly and found her way under the sheets. I lay there again on my back, left arm behind my head, and the other wrapped around her, as we gazed into the blackness of the sky, watching the snowflakes fall now heavy and wet, into oblivion. The blue-white light of the streetlamp outside my window illuminating her pale skin, with the sound of my Melody sweetly playing in my mind. We lay there for half an hour, silent, breathing rhythmically, completely in tune to each other as the night bled away and our eyes sank without protest behind their heavy lids; laying there peacefully in our silent serenity.

Morning light flooded the window, and I woke up alone. There was a part of me that believed the entire night had been a dream. I rubbed my eyes and looked out my window at the ground that showed little to no signs of having been snowed on, and my bed was as cold as when I had climbed in the previous night. I flung myself around so that my feet were dangling off of the bed. I picked myself up onto my shoulders and dropped my weight onto the floor, landing on a wet plastic bag, a very cold, wet plastic bag.

I gathered myself up and crept down the stairs and into the kitchen to find Mom making some breakfast. I poured myself some orange juice and wished her a happy new year with a kiss on the cheek. She turned and with a little bit of orneriness in her voice said:

"Sounds like it started off OK for you…"

I was initially shocked at the thought of my mother knowing that Melody had stayed most of the night with me, paralyzed, I forced out a quick and breathy "yeah…"

After a brief and harrowing series of seconds she said that she heard Max and Melody leave close to 5 this morning. I sighed internally and with a chuckle in my voice let Mom know that time got away from us. To which she let me know that I need not let that happen too often. I assured her that it was a special occasion being New Year's and all and appreciated not being in trouble. A quick smooch on her cheek and I (along with my juice) made it back up the stairs to stare out the window at my neighbor's house, Melody's three soft words still echoing in my ears.

Max was there, waiting, pacing. He looked like hell, but I suppose we all did by that point. He rushed to me and threw his arms around me, supporting the back of my head with his left hand like I was a baby again, too weak to be able to support the weight of my head. I remember that because of how much I appreciated it. He was sobbing, heaving tears onto the shoulder of my hospital gown, hours and hours of suspense and unanswered calls having proven to be a hefty weight. After a few moments we separated;

"How did you get here?" I asked.

"I got word about the wreck and left early, one of the other counselors is covering my bunks for me."

"I'm sorry." This was the first time I had attempted to verbalize my guilt.

"No, there's no need...I'm glad you are OK."

"I don't know about that yet."

"Dad," Max turned his father, "where's Melody?"

Dr. Black told Max that she just got out of surgery and is still under sedation, but that her vitals are holding. Max sank, understanding that such a terrible statement is what would have to pass for good news.

"Can I see her?" Max asked.

Dr. Black turned to his wife and nodded,

"Your mother will take you to see her, but son," he paused, "you won't exactly know what you are seeing...she's...bandaged up pretty good."

Max nodded toward his father, acknowledging the statement and preparing himself for the shock to come.

I returned to my hospital room and sat up on the bed. The room filled with my parents, Dr. Black, and after a few minutes of silence, two police officers and a young woman dressed in obnoxiously bright clothing and a white lab-coat.

"Sam, I'm Dr. Gould, one of the psychologists on staff. I wanted to be present with these two officers while you gave your statement, just to observe and take some initial impressions, is that alright with you?" She ended with a smile and slight tilt over her right shoulder.

"Yes."

"Ok."

Before the police officers were able to begin, Melody's dad started in on them;

"What's going to happen to the guy who did this?"

"We are here to ask Sam a few questions about last night."

"Answer me, dammit."

"Sir, we need to speak with Sam, if you want to stay in the room then you need to stop talking."

Silence again.

"Now Sam, do you remember what happened last night?"

"Some."

"Start at the beginning, tell us anything you remember from last night."

"I remember Melody and I had been at her parent's house, celebrating our engagement...we had dinner, played a few card games...."

"What time was that?" interrupted one of the officers, Jones on his name-tag.

I looked at Dr. Black,

"I dunno, 6:45, maybe 7?"

Dr. Black nodded in agreement, the cops didn't notice.

"And then what?" continued Jones.

"And then...we left...maybe around 9 or so, it was barely light out. We walked to my car, I was going to take Melody to her apartment before I went back to mine. I opened her door, she climbed in...I closed her door and got in on my side. She looked at me and asked if we could drive around for a few. We drove around a little while and stopped at the park."

"Why would you stop at the park that late in the evening?"

"That park is important to us, we have a lot of memories there," I could feel my eyes bolting and jotting from side to side as I searched my memory for anything I could piece together, "we went there a lot ever since we were kids. We were just gonna sit there on the swings like we always did, talk maybe...I dunno...we were just there."

"Anything else?"

"Yeah, of course...sorry...I stopped the car at the park, got out and started walking around the front to go open her door," at that point I stopped, the memory of that exact moment filling me, killing me. My eyes flooded as I tried to move past the memory, tried to voice the things I was seeing in my mind to officers, but I was stuck...I couldn't even breathe. My mother moved over towards me and put her hand on my back, soothing me out of my frozen state.

"I was walking around to get her door and that is when it happened, that's when the other vehicle came." I looked up, first at the officers and then at Dr. Gould, her face now expressing concern.

"That's the moment. I was to the side of the car, in front of the passenger side when the SUV hit us...her...hit her...I don't think I was hit, I'm not sure what these scratches and bruises are from."

"Anything else?" Jones' voice dry and impatient.

"No...I woke up here in this bed."

"When the ambulance arrived," Dr. Gould began, "you were found only a few feet from Melody, you were unconscious, do you know what happened?"

"No, I'm sorry I don't."

"Ok," Jones stated, "I think we've got everything we need," as he motioned toward the door.

"What's going to happen to the guy who did this, officer?" Dr. Black returned to his earlier impatient tone.

Jones turned back to him and simply replied, "I think we've got everything we need."

Dr. Gould brought herself over to my bed and sat down, facing me, "How are you feeling, Sam?"

"How am I feeling?"

"Yeah...physically...mentally...any of it."

"I don't know how I feel...just...torn...between a lot of things."

"They are wanting to release you today...soon in fact."

"OK."

"Do you feel alright to leave?"

"Sure."

"Is there anything you want to talk about?"

"I don't know...I don't think so...if there is...I'll talk to my folks, or Melody's."

"I think you should. I'm going to recommend that you see a counselor at some point in the next few weeks."

"For what?"

"Grief, guilt, anger, or just to talk about anything you are going through, anything extra you may remember, or if you're feeling stressed or confused...anything."

"Wait...how long are you thinking it's going to take Melody to recover?"

Dr. Gould was silent.

"Longer than weeks?"

"We don't know, Sam."

"She's going to be ok, though, right? I mean yeah she's been through all this but she out of surgery and all that, right?"

"She is."

"So...she's gonna be fine then, right?"

"Sam...We just don't know yet."

Dr. Gould stood up and looked around the room, she apologized for something and left. I was still stunned at the thought that Melody would be stuck in this hospital for any real length of time. I looked up at my father, his face showing concern and worry, Mom's was the same way. I looked over to Dr. Black, fighting back tears as he slowly walked out to the hallway, hoping soon for his wife and son to return to him.

Max and Mrs. Black had come back to my hospital room, both clearly shaken. Dr. Black turned to me and let me know that they were going to head home to gather a few things so that they could come back for the night. He told us that the next few days would tell us a lot and that they wanted to have someone here at all times in case there are any changes. Max came over to me and gave me a hug.

"Thank God you weren't in there too."

"What?"

"With her, in the car."

I know Max's intent was honest and pure and kind, but at that moment I was overcome with a sense of self-loathing that would only grow over the next several months. I again was unable to breathe, and as Max looked me in the eyes, all I could do was subtly nod at his sentiment.

I was released from the hospital a few hours later. As we entered the elevator I told my dad I wanted to see Melody before we left, he told me that wouldn't be a good idea. He told me I needed to focus first on my healing and making sure that I was whole enough to be able to support her as she went through whatever she was going to go through.

"What am I supposed to do?"

"I don't know, Sam...let's take you home, first."

"No, I don't want to go back to my place yet..."

"Don't worry, son, you're coming home with us."

The elevator door opened and we headed out the lobby of the hospital, my mother and I waited as dad went to pull the car around. I was there with them, leaving, not knowing how to show protest against them when all I wanted was to rush back in and be by the side of my fiancée. Dad pulled up and mom grabbed my hand and started walking, my body disconnected from my heart, from my mind and from my will, walking without any sign of hesitation away from her, from Melody. I sat in the back seat as the car door closed, my eyes fixated on the hospital, and slowly we drove away...leaving her alone.

Whether it was the stress or any number of other things, I couldn't keep my eyes open and had begun to doze as we drove home, the car quietly humming to me in the backseat, bumps and potholes gently rocking me into a light sleep. The sun beat down through the windows as my closed eyes stared up into the bright blue heavens. I had been out of it for maybe half an hour by the time we pulled into the drive. I opened my eyes and the world had taken on a different hue. I pulled my head up from the headrest and looked left to the Black household, their driveway was empty and the lights in the house were all off. We all knew that the family had returned to the hospital to be by Melody's side, and perhaps it was because of that that the emptiness of the house seemed so scary.

"Dad," I said, "I need to go back...this isn't right without her."

"Sammy," he began, "it'll be OK. You need to rest and find some sort of foothold on what has happened before you can go back."

"Foothold?"

"Yeah...your life...all of our lives have changed, you were unconscious for a big part of that, and you need to take the time to realize what has happened and cope with it. If you don't do that...you won't be any good to her when you do go back...and she needs you to be strong for her right now. So trust us, get some rest, and we will talk about everything tomorrow."

There were no more conversations between us that night, only thoughts and short sentiments put forward, but never exchanged. We climbed out of the car and headed toward the front door of the house. As I walked behind my parents, all I could think about was her, and how she was in pain, and that there was nothing I could do to help, and that I was heading home to rest.

I closed the door behind me and could smell the old familiar smell of home, it was the closest thing to comfort that I had felt since waking up in that hospital bed. It was evening and I was exhausted, but not the least bit tired. There would be no dinner that night, no television shows worth watching, nothing would be as it had been. We all just milled around the place, from room to room, sometimes crossing paths and sometimes not. The only words I heard at all from either of my folks was simply:

"Sam, we're glad you're OK," or "We're so thankful you're home with us."

The stigma of what had happened to Melody followed us all as we wandered aimless through the doors and hallways of our home. It was not until I gave in to the truth that there would be no escaping the pain and fear of what happened that I was able to resign myself to the idea of going to bed. So badly I had wanted to remove myself from that pain and from that fear, so badly I wanted to leave it somewhere in the house, so that I could pick it back up tomorrow and carry it then...but I could not shake it, I could not drop it. I stared at the first step on the way to my bedroom before calling out,

"Mom...Dad...I love you guys, thanks for coming to get me."

They both came to the stairs.

"If you need us at all, any time, please just let us know...we're right here."

I worked my way up the stairs and down the hallway to my room. I opened the door and saw my bed; neatly made and sitting level to the window sill, having never been taken down. The blinds were pulled up and as I crawled on top of my comforter, I could look through to Melody's old window, she was not there, and despite it all, I prayed and begged for her light to flip on and her beautiful smile to come rushing to that window as it had so many times before.

I felt nothing laying there in silence. I was numb. Cliché as it may sound. I knew what had happened, what I had been through and what everyone else must be going through as well. I knew that I loved Melody and I hated that she had to have been in so much unbearable pain, but I didn't cry, I couldn't. I lay there, trying to turn my mind off, trying to not think about anything that had happened in the past 32 hours...trying not to realize that I could no longer get to the person I loved the most in life if I wanted...that she had been removed from me. There was no sleep, there was no hiding from realizations, and even so, there were no tears.

I lay there on my bed, staring again to the sky, now black from storm clouds that moved in as the sun had set. Raindrops slowly began to fall on my window, flashes of lighting and crashes of thunder spread through the night sky. I remembered, laying there in my bed, a storm from years ago. It would have been 4 months after the first time she had said 'I love you.' April. There was a tremendous storm on the way to town, and both mine and Melody's folks had left town for a few days to attend a conference in Phoenix or someplace like that.

Melody had come over to watch the storm with me. We hadn't planned on more than laying on my bed, in the same way that I was doing now, watching as the rain fell to the earth. Melody had commented, I remember, that the whole day had felt sad, and the harsh rain was a suiting end.

Her hand would grab mine, mine would hold hers; we would look at each other for a few minutes then tear ourselves and our hands away to watch the rain. Hours flew by into the night and still the storm persisted. Glances turned into stares, kisses turned into intimate embraces. Thunder and lightning became stronger, louder, more ferocious, and everything happening outside of that window, all of the intense, chaotic, passionate power of the storm was being echoed and matched inside the walls of my bedroom, confined to the thin and sweat drenched layers of my bed sheets. I would embarrass us both if I were to go further into details at this point, but the love that flowed from Melody that night was beyond any magnificent feeling that I had or have since to encounter.

The night ended, the night of the storm, the night we first made love, ended with a soft kiss and Melody and I creaking down the stairs to the front door. Our night ended with her lips by my ear, telling me that she loved me. My night ended with a smile and a shaky ascent back into my warm, wet, and now empty bed.

With that memory, I began to cry. Tears fell from my cheeks in the same way rain fell from the clouds, my sobs as booming as the thunder, my spirit broken as the darkness split by lightning.

Hours past and my cheeks dried, exhausted but still restless. I found my way to my bathroom in the hopes that some NyTime would be in my medicine cabinet. I found the red liquid and began to drink. I finished the quarter of a bottle and returned to bed. Medicated sleep coursed through me and this was the beginning of my undoing.

I woke up in the early afternoon from the liquid-induced sleep feeling shaky and thirstier than I ever remember being. I sat up and stared out from my window into Melody's old room, wishing as I had the night before for there to be any movement, any anything, but I received nothing. I threw on some sweats and made my way downstairs, I made it to the bottom of the stairs with weak knees, greeted by the somber image of my folks and Melody's parents in the living room.

"Son." My dad started in.

Fear started in me early that day, my mind immediately going to the last place I wanted it to go. That same fear must have crawled to my expression as my dad continued:

"Melody's OK...but there have been some complications."

"Dad, just tell me!

"After everything that has happened, the wreck, the trauma, the blood loss, all of it...Melody is in a coma."

I looked around with panic shining through my eyes like a light from a lighthouse, scanning the room for any ships of hope, there were none.

"A coma?

"Yes," Dr. Black picked up, "her vitals have begun to even out and more than likely she will continue to become more and more stable over the next few days, but she isn't waking up yet."

"Yet?"

"All the medicines from the surgery are out of her system but she hasn't come to yet, she is still unconscious and from what we can tell...unresponsive."

"How long will she stay that way?" Pain and anger cracked through my voice as my eyes watered and my chin quivered?

"How long will she be...gone?"

Heavy, suffocating silence.

"We don't know, son."

"Are they keeping her-" I began.

"Yes," Dr. Black interrupted, "she is being taken care of, and we are going to give her as much time as she needs to come back to us." His voice now ripe with fear and sadness for the loss of his daughter.

"I have to go see her."

"Sam, that's probably not best just yet."

"I'm not asking, dad, Melody needs me and I need to be there with her, she needs to know I'm there."

"Son...-"

"-No Dad. I refuse to believe that the best thing is for me to stay away from my wife."

"She's not-"

"Don't you dare, not right now dad...I'm going, whether its with you, or her folks, or Max or if I have to walk there myself; I am going to go see her!"

Angry, hateful, back-against-the-wall silence.

I left the room to get a glass of water, the strain from arguing and stress had dried my throat even further. By the time I came returned to the living room everyone was seated. I sat on the arm of the couch, finishing my water.

"When can we go?"

"You need to eat."

"I'm not hungry."

"You can choke down a sandwich, your body needs it. Throw on some clothes, your mother will make you a sandwich and then we will head to the hospital."

"OK, thank you."

I turned away to head up the stairs,

"Sam..." Dr. Black said.

"It won't be easy to see her like this."

I nodded and continued on my way up to my old room to find some jeans.

I found my clothes from the day before and slid them on as I stumbled to the bathroom. I popped open the mirror above the sink to grab my toothbrush and deodorant. Mom always kept a fresh toothbrush behind there for me in case I came home but apparently still unable to cope with the idea of buying her baby boy deodorant. All that was left was an old bottle of dad's cologne, the same as I used that night several years ago. I cupped some water in my hands to wash my face and slick back my hair, fighting off memories. I began to realize that the more I looked around the more memories I had to fight off. She was everywhere, memories of Melody covered every inch of my life both old and new, and the more those memories crept into my head the more they felt just like that...memories.

The ride to the hospital was a surreal one. I mean, never-mind that I was going to visit the person I loved most in life and who in a short number of months was supposed to be my wife, the two men that I looked up to the most, my father and hers were completely silent, unable to find words to describe or even fit the moment. I suppose it was best that way, these silent and terrible moments on the way to the hospital would be nothing compared to the horrible ones to come.

We arrived at the hospital a little after 2 in the afternoon. Melody's dad lead the way to the 5th floor ICU, she had been turfed there from the lower level she had been when I found her the day before. We exited the elevator, her dad still leading us with a fast and nervous pace. I followed as close as I could, my legs had been replaced with heavy weights. Winding around a few corridors and pushing past waiting rooms full of anxious families, I caught up to our fathers, both standing outside of the room, sullen expressions tracing their faces. We stood there and we waited for the nurse that was checking in on Melody to come out and tell us it would be OK to go in. She grabbed at Melody, maneuvered parts of her; stared at the machines Melody was hooked up to, wrote some things down and continued on. Standing there watching had been one of the most challenging things I had ever done. I stood there with my heart pounding in my throat, the sight of Melody unable to respond to the poking and the prodding was more than I could handle....I needed so badly to rush into that room and tell her that I was there and that everything would be fine...even if I didn't believe it.

The nurse let us know that it was OK to go in as she was leaving and that she would tell Melody's doctor that we were here. Melody's dad stood at the door and told me he and my dad would wait out in the hall until the doctor showed up. I went in slowly, the anxiety and desire that came with waiting outside had left and the weights had returned to my legs. I stood in that doorway, listening to the beeps of the machines and gasping noises of ventilators that surround the areas as I focused solely on remembering how to walk.

From the time I woke up in that hospital and realized that something terrible had happened to the moment that was currently surrounding me, nothing had seemed real; nothing had felt actual. Even as I stood over her body, watching as she lie motionless on that bed, none of it seemed real. It wasn't until I touched her for the first time that the walls of disbelief came crashing down around me. I looked her over quizzically, almost as if I didn't understand what she was doing there in that bed. My eyes fixated on her face, without much thought I grabbed her hand with mine, it remained limp and lifeless, and I knew at that moment, I understood that she wasn't there with me, she had been removed to some place that I could not follow, some place that I could not be with her, and I understood that she was gone.

"Mel?" My voice strained through worn-out emotion.

"Melody?"

I lost sight of her from behind a wall of tears. The water streamed down my face as my eyes shut harder than they ever had with the hopes that hers would open when mine did.

"Melody?"

The doctor entered the room with both dads in tow.

"Son," he began, "her surgery went well, we were able to stop the bleeding, but loss of blood coupled with severe trauma has caused her to lapse into a coma."

"A coma." Saying the words made no sense to me at that moment, and were strictly to let the doctor know that I was listening, even if I wasn't able to pay a moment's attention. My eyes stayed on Melody throughout his speech.

"Yes," he continued, "we have been running some basic diagnostic tests to see what areas of her brain may be damaged, but so far she has been mostly unresponsive to any sort of stimuli. We have been able to control the swelling in her cranium, but the lasting effects will remain unknown until her condition evolves."

"Evolves into what," her dad asked.

"Well...the tests we have administered physically show that while there may be some damage to the cerebral cortex; her brain stem, which regulates heart rate, respiration, etc. remains unharmed, but again there are still several tests to run and scans that we won't take until some of the effects of the surgery are lessened and her body has been allowed to heal as much as it can on its own."

"Will she come out of it?" The pressing and obvious question had to be asked.

"We don't know, son. She could come out of it, but we can't guarantee anything at this point. She could wake up at any time and be fine, but more than likely, IF she does wake up, there is some damage that will have lasting effects. Again we don't know what those effects may be or even the extent to which they would manifest. All we can do is monitor and continue running tests for any sort of awareness she may have, see if her condition improves, stays the same or worsens."

"How long will it take to find out more?"

"The next several days will tell us quite a bit. In patients that are comatose due to severe trauma, the longer the patient remains comatose the odds of recovery becomes increasingly smaller. As I said, her body will begin to heal itself from the collision and the surgery, and we will become more confident in conducting scans and running more tests."

"And in the meantime?

"Sam-" Dad started in.

"Pray, be together, support each other...whatever your family does in times like these," were the doctor's words.

Those words resonated in the air for all of us. For the first time we were, as a group, referred to as a whole...as a family, a macabre reminder of the beauty that was supposed to come in the next few months. I had no idea what it was that we 'as a family' did in times like these; nothing like this had ever happened.

The doctor's closing words were simply that he had to go take care of a few other patients but that he would keep Dr. Black up to date on everything that was to come. Dr. Black thanked him and joined me at Melody's side. He put his hand on my shoulder in an attempt to be reassuring, his silence an attempt at stoicism.

"She's going to be OK, Sam," my father, still near the door claimed.

"Dr. Black...do you remember what you told me the night of the accident before Melody and I left?"

"To call me Emmett," he said dryly.

"Sorry, no, the other thing Emmett."

"I guess not, what was that?"

"You told me that the key to a successful marriage was to grow together, to change together. Do you remember?"

"Sam," his voice began in protest before letting out a sigh, "yes, I remember."

"I don't know how to do that now."

"There's nothing you can do but be supportive, be here with her, and take care of yourself like she would want and expect of you."

"I will. I will be here every day, and I won't leave her side until I absolutely have to, but she's gone through so much, and I can't go through it with her, she's on her own, no matter how close I am...I can't do this with her."

We stood there in silence for a while. I couldn't tear my eyes away from her. I studied her, learned the new scars on her face and neck and arms...I learned the new landscape of her features. My father eventually sat down, Dr. Black...Emmett brought me a chair as he pulled on up on the other side of the bed. I couldn't sit. Every bit of my nervous energy was devoted to staring at her, waiting for her to open her eyes. I would stare at her and try to think logically about what had happened and what was to come, but my mind kept returning to the thought that people can tell when they are being stared at by someone, and that soon she would feel my stare and open her eyes, just to tell me to stop.

The hours crept by, Max and Mrs. Black...Suzanne came by. There was no meaningful conversation between us. Emmett would hold her and Max would switch between my side and the opposite side of Melody's bed. Emmett and my dad left to get some dinner, the others offered to stay with me, but I asked for some time alone with my fiancée. I realize how incredibly rude it must have been for me to ask Melody's mom and brother to leave, but I told them I needed to be alone with her...to experience that. They were gracious enough to grant me my request and let me know they would be back before too long with some food.

I had been alone with Melody for maybe 5 or 10 minutes before having the courage to speak to her. I took a seat on the edge of the bed, having set her hand back down at her side. I put my hand on the side of her face just as she had that New Year's night.

"I love you," were the only words I could think of at that moment. I moved my hand from her cheek and began to slowly and delicately run my fingers through her hair.

Silence. Beeping, mechanical silence.

"I'm right here, love. Don't you worry about a thing, OK? Every-thing's going to be OK, you just rest up," tears now forming again in my eyes, "you just rest up and focus on getting better, OK? Don't you worry about anything."

I leaned forward, hovering over her, covering her face in my shadow. I lowered my lips to her forehead and kissed her gently before again whispering "I love you, Melody."

I began to sit back up and closed my eyes, causing a tear to fall and land on her cheek. I wouldn't have believed it had it not happened to me, but with that tear, her heart monitor stopped. It didn't flat-line, it didn't skip, it just stopped. My eyes remained closed and I couldn't move. I remained perfectly still, hoping against hope that when I opened my eyes, somehow she would be staring at me as I had been at her for the past several hours. I had stopped breathing but could no longer hold my breath. My eyes shot open as I took in my first breath, and with that breath the illusion of hope had again been shattered, the heart monitor resuming its pace, and the feeling of loneliness returning to my chest.

A couple of weeks had gone by with no changes in her condition. She remained stable and though her body had been healing the way the doctor's had hoped, she remained far away from me. I did exactly as I said I would and was at her side most of the hours of the day. Work had allowed me to use my vacation time on short notice and I had accumulated enough to last for a few weeks. My family knew that I would be the hospital at any given moment and began showing up there to check on me, and Melody, whenever they began to worry. I saw the Black family even more as they came to see their daughter frequently. Max was struggling the most of them. He became restless with his sister's inability to wake up and often came by with a mixtape full of music he knew Melody would hate. He would bring it and a player and sit on the other side of her from me and make us listen to it, hoping she would get 'annoyed out of her coma.'

August began and Max struggled with his decision to return to college. After the three of us had finished our 4 years at a nearby University, Max decided to continue on in his father's footsteps and become a Chiropractor. He wanted badly to finish his degree but was torn about leaving his sister behind. His doctor school was only about an hour away, but Max didn't want to be any further away than his parent's house if things with Melody developed one way or another.

Melody's parents would come and read to her or give her updates on what was happening in their lives. One thing I always loved about hearing her parents speak to her was that they hadn't reverted to speaking to her as if she were a child again. They spoke to her in loving tones, but tones that respected her and supported her in her situation. Her father would talk about how proud he was of her and how he wanted to take her places they had always talked about going. Her mother would tell her that she should take her time and heal, but to always remember that they were there for her whenever she might need them. Both spoke to her as though it would be her choice to wake up, and that whenever she was ready, we would all go home.

Mostly I would just sit there and hold her hand and watch her body for any sign of change. I knew the slope of her feet and the angles of her head. I had become accustomed to the new scars she would have. The worst was on the left side of her face; it stretched from just under her hairline to the top of her cheekbone. We all knew that when she woke up she would be pissed about it and it became something of a running source of humor around this incredibly sad and morbid situation.

I wish I could say that when I did speak to her it was hopeful or pleasant or supportive. I tried to be those things for her as often as I could, but mostly when I spoke, I was apologetic. I had a difficult time even forming words around her without tears, not just from sadness but from a tremendous sense of guilt. In our silence together, all those hours, I had become able to remember every moment of the wreck. I would sit there holding her hand as the thoughts of the crash shot through my mind, the sounds of metals colliding, the rush of displaced air crossing my face as the bullet sent from the dark of night crashed through and damaged her. At first it took everything I had to keep those thoughts out of my head, but as the days have worn on, I came to immerse myself in them, realizing that this would be my punishment for not protecting the most precious thing in my world.

In those first weeks I lost so much more than just her, I lost my appetite, I lost sleep, I lost myself. After submitting to the guilt, I began dreaming about the wreck, and that is how I came to remember so much of it. At first it was quick shards of light rushing past me, or I'd close my eyes and hear the explosion from the collision and be jolted awake. But before long it became a reenactment of the scene; sometimes I would close my eyes and remember the sound of my shoes on the pavement as I walked around the car to let her out, or I could smell the night air or I could see her smile through the windshield change into an expression of fear as the SUV came barreling towards her.

I had been haunted by those images at all time of the day, but the dreams were always so much more vivid and painful, and whenever I could avoid sleep, I certainly would.

I had become used to the schedule the nursing staff had been assigned too. They would come and move Melody in the late afternoon, rub her muscles and try to stimulate any part of her that otherwise might atrophy. Late evenings would be cleanings and a changing of the bed sheets, both to help prevent bedsores. Each evening the routine remained as it always had, on schedule and tremendously heart-wrenching.

It was in the middle of my second week of visits that my mother came to the room alone to visit us. She had concern written all over her face and sincerity infused into every word she was able to muster through.

"Son, you need to come home."

"She needs me, Mom."

"She...she needs you to be strong and to take care of yourself. She needs you to let her do whatever it is she needs to do."

"I can't, I won't leave her to do this alone."

"What is it you are hoping to help her with, Sam!?"

"I...I dunno, but I do know that if I were there in that bed-"

"She would come and support you, but she would keep being strong and living her life."

"I was going to say if I were in that bed I would want her here."

"Then you are more selfish than we raised you to be."

I looked up at her through hurt eyes, those words of hers, laced with sincerity, cut me as deeply as some of the wounds on Melody.

"Mom? I can't. When I go back to my place my mind is still right here in this chair. When I try to eat, all I can think about is the pain she must be in. When I sleep, all I see is her, all I see is what happened and there's nothing I can do about it, nothing I can change about ANY of this...but being here...sitting here...at least we are together."

"Sam, come home with me. Let me cook you a warm dinner, your dad wants to see you and it'll do you good to spend an evening outside of the hospital walls."

"Mom...I don't-"

"Sammy...this isn't up for debate...come home...I'll bring you back tomorrow if that is what you want."

I sat there, moved by the concern and love that came from my mother's best effort at 'tough love' before nodding to her in acceptance.

"OK, Mom."

I looked to Melody, grabbed her hand in mine and told her that I loved her and that I would be back the next day.

I stood and turned toward my mother, she remained motionless as though I was a wounded pup that had just started to warm up to the offer of her aid, as though the slightest movement on her part would force me to abort the decision I had made to go home, as though if she moved, I would return to my chair at Melody's side and remain there for some indeterminate amount of time.

I smiled as much of a smile as I could and said, "Let's go home."

She returned my smile as we gathered up the few items I had brought with me from my apartment and we started toward the path that would lead me back home to a nice place and the comfort of my parents.

We sat there at the dinner table, my folks and I, existing in the silence of uncertainty. Each of us undoubtedly with a list of things we wanted to talk about but each unsure how to begin and each of us hoping that if we were to start in on some important conversation that the phone would ring with some news...any news.

Halfway through the meal my dad found the courage to start in:

"Have you been back in to work, Sam?"

"Not yet, I had a lot of time off saved up..."

"You shouldn't use it all."

"Oh?" I said, largely a courtesy since I hadn't spoken to him in a week's time.

"No. You'll need it for your honeymoon." His words coming off only slightly backhanded. I knew that he meant well and his words were said with the hope of buoying my spirits.

"Yeah? You really think so?" Everyone's hearts had been broken enough lately, I didn't want to get into an argument with him about his failing attempt at thoughtfulness. In a way I appreciated the sentiment but couldn't fully indulge in its comforts, and to lead on that the same spirit he was working to fix had already been shattered beyond repair would have only lead to more pain for him...pain I couldn't be around to help him cope with right now.

"I do. I think Melody will be up and running around again before we know it."

"Me too, dear." Mother chimed in through a tight-lipped, nervous smile as she quickly batted her eyes at me.

I nodded in the exact same way as I had been so often for the past few weeks, but all I could think to myself was "I bet I'd clean up if I ever played these two at poker." Call me callous...but it was the truth.

I lost myself to a stare as the thought had entered my head, but I could feel both of my parents watching me, waiting for some sort of word or gesture from me to agree with them, to tell them that I believed Melody was going to return to us soon. God I wanted so badly to believe that, I wished that I would have been able to even fake some sort of agreement. I had been around her motionless body too much and I had spoken to her too many words that went unanswered and couldn't bring myself even to say 'Yeah, I'm sure she'll be fine." Thankfully I wouldn't have to, the doorbell rang, it was Max; he let himself in.

"Max," I said with a sign of relief in my voice, "Hey....how ya doin', man?"

Confused by the scene Max continued in from the door, "Hey...am I interrupting?"

"No no, of course not, whatcha up to?"

"Not too much, I went to see Melody and you weren't there. I came home from the hospital and saw you guys through the window and thought that I would come say hi...I feel like I haven't seen you in forever."

"Umm...yeah. Mom coaxed me into coming home for some food and rest...how've you been."

Max looked as though he had something on his mind that he was just dying to get out, but the nervous looks he would shoot at my parents before speaking told me he wanted to talk in private.

"I've been OK....how have you been?"

I turned away from Max toward my folks. I excused myself and told them that Max and I were going to go up to my room for a bit and to holler for me if they needed us. They smiled and nodded in sync.

Max and I headed up to my room as I fought past the memories that were trying so hard to burrow into my mind of all the times the three of us would have ran up to my room as kids. Back then, if I had tried to leave in the middle of a meal to play with Max and Melody there would have been disapproving looks and lectures about manners, but I guess it helped that weren't leaving the table to go play in my room.

We entered my room and I turned to sit on my bed. As I sat I could see Max's charade of strength wash away. I quickly rushed to him and wrapped my arms around him as he began to cry. He buried his eyes into my collarbone as his body heaved sobs into mine. We stood there for several minutes until he was able to compose himself again. I was still too stunned at his collapse to respond in any sort of meaningful way. Max pulled away and I lowered my head as we stood at arm's length to try and meet his sullen stare.

"Max?"

"I'm sorry man...I just...I don't know what I'm doing."

"Don't be sorry. None of us really know what to do anymore."

"No...My folks, they are trying too hard to keep their heads up and to keep moving forward. It's so hard to watch my family try and exist without her. I get so mad because there are times when it feels like they aren't worried...like they don't care."

Max's words were becoming increasingly difficult to understand as the emotion in his voice would rise and fall with his breathing. One of the most heart-wrenching things to witness is a grown man crying, utterly bawling and broken down. Max continued "I know they care, they love Melody just like they love me...but to not talk about it...to not wallow in the fact that 25% of the family is laying in a hospital...it seems so wrong. They go to see her like once a day, but that's it. "

"What do you want 'em to do, Max?"

"I don't know...something...anything. I mean, I know we can't all just sit at her bedside 24/7 like you do..."

"Something wrong with supporting her?" I interjected, mildly offended.

"No...It's just...opposites. My family is acting like they've already moved on...like they've given up and forgotten or like it's no big deal at all...and you...you seem as though the world has completely stopped...like there is no moving on...like your life has ended."

Silence lingered between us as Max paused for a few moments to regain his composure and wipe tears away from his eyes and cheeks.

"It's just that my parents went off one deep end you and you've gone off the other."

Max shook his head as he looked to the floor. "I just didn't know that when she left, everyone else would too."

"Max...of course I'm still here for you...I've just been going through a lot. I know we all have, and yeah, maybe we each have our own ways of dealing with it...but never think for a moment that you can't come to me when something is wrong."

"Everything is wrong, Sam."

"I know it is."

"Do you?! I get why you are always there with her...but until I showed up at your door and lost my shit crying on your shoulder...did you have any clue that I wasn't coping so well?"

"Nobody is coping Max! Right now we are stranded between hope and fear. Hell, nobody saw this coming...nobody knows how to deal with this when it happens. You see your folks as having moved on already but I guarantee you that's not the case...I know your folks almost as well as you do so surely you can see that they are just trying to be strong for you right now."

"I don't need strong! I need people to be as scared as I am, to let me know that even if we are scared to death and even if she doesn't come outta this that things are going to be OK!"

"How can you say that? In what way will things be 'OK'? How can you want to accept the idea of her dying?!"

"I'm not! God knows I don't want that! No one wants that but it's a reality. She may come out of this fine, she may come back to us with some damage, but she might die! I'm the only one trying to deal with that and it feels lonely!"

"The only one?! Max I sit there with her for hours a day! You're there for what...an hour every now and then?"

"So it's a contest?"

"No it's not a contest...but don't you dare stand there and tell me, the one that loves Melody more than ANYthing else in this world that I'm not going through this too."

"Sam, you sit in the room with her...what...talking and thinking, praying? What do you do that's so important to her? Do you really think that she would want you wallowing and sitting there crying over her?"

There was silence again as his words hung in the air. I had a long list of very nasty things I wanted to say to him, but I knew that if I waited, remained silent he would recant those past thoughts as an attempt to be hurtful.

More silence.

"You know I'm right, Sammy."

Those were certainly not the words I expected him to follow up with. His next words continued to strike at me without mercy, even if it hadn't been his intention, but it was through the harsh points he attempted to make that I began to look within myself for some reason as to my reaction to the whole wreck-and-coma thing.

"What you're doing...I know you see it as support...but at the center of it all it's you being selfish."

I looked at Max as though he had grabbed hold of a raw and naked nerve and began to pull.

I had no retort, no response for the verbal bitch-slap that had just landed. Instead I turned and walked back over to my bed, mind racing to explain to myself that Max was wrong. He picked back up.

"You are there with her because you don't know where else to be. We all feel displaced right now...nowhere seems like it should without Melody...NO where. Yes I hate it that it feels like mom and dad have moved on already, and maybe you're right in that it's just a show to help me feel safe, but at least they are PRETENDING to have worked through everything...you've stopped Sam, you've stopped living."

Silence again. I gave up on waiting for an apology from Max, maybe he just needed a whipping boy, someone to yell at for a few without the fear of guilt or judgment, maybe that was the best way to be there for him right now. Max came and sat next to me on the bed.

"Tell me I'm wrong."

"You are," I tore my stare from the floor to his face, "you are wrong."

"Then tell me about it. Tell me how I'm wrong. I see you sitting next to her whenever I go to visit but you hardly speak to anyone anymore."

"I dunno...I just...there's something there in the silence," these and the following words were my first insight to what I had been thinking and feeling over the past few weeks. It took the confrontation with Max to draw it out of me, and maybe these next moments should have been the first indication that I needed some help...but I didn't see it that way, and even if he did, God bless him he never said it.

"When I speak to her...there is no answer...no response. When I hold her hand she can't hold mine. I look at her lying in that bed and I realize over and over a million times a day that I have no clue what she is going through...what she has already been through. She lays there and I watch for any sign of movement. I watch for any flutter behind her eyelids to tell me she is dreaming...to show me she is still in there. I look at the scars on her body, on her face and I realize she is changing, has changed...and I wasn't able to help her through it. But sitting there in that silence...where we just exist together...that is when I feel the most connected to her. I sit there and I can feel her...I like to believe that she can feel me too."

This had been the most I had been able to speak about Melody without being reduced to tears. Considering that this was the closest thing to an emotional or psychological breakthrough that I had had since the accident...I should have been more proud or excited to have gained the extra insight...but I felt little, there would be no catharsis from this confession, from this revelation.

"I see her scars and I know they will always be there. I watch her as she sleeps and I know she will remain that way until she is able to return to me...I listen to her silence and I return it, my only way of communicating and connecting with her."

"Sam," Max started. I looked at him waiting for his next words to rebuke mine. My expectation for apology had shifted into one of reprehension.

"Ya gotta come back to us. I've decided not to go back to school this semester. I'm gonna need you to help me through all of this while we wait for her to come back. I want to help you through whatever it is you're going to go through, 'cuz you don't gotta go through it alone."

"I kinda do."

"How's that?"

"Because it was my fault, Max."

"You're the only one that believes that."

"I know."

"There was nothing you could have done. There was no way you could have stopped what happened."

"Maybe not...but I wasn't even in the car...all I could do was watch as it happened...and no matter how many times I hear everyone try to minimize it...I am guilty."

No one blames you."

"Maybe that's the problem."

"What's that supposed to mean."

This was the moment of dreadful clarity.

"Maybe I feel the need to be forgiven...but what do you when you feel that way and no one feels there is anything to be forgiven for?"

"Apparently you torture yourself needlessly."

My eyes shot from one side of their sockets to the other as I began to process the words I had said and the words I had heard. They gelled together and began to resonate with the words from Max's father. "The only way to change is together."

It was there in that moment that I began to conceive what it was that I would go on to do...it was then that I stood in front of the door that lead to this damned path that inspired my destruction.

Another couple of weeks passed. There still had been no progress from Melody but then again she hadn't gotten any worse. I, on the other hand, had progress both in my ability to return to what others might call 'everyday life' and my inability to cope with the guilt that I had finally been able to identify through my conversation with Max. I had returned to my job and tried to bury myself in the design layouts that the magazine would need. I did my best to ignore the silence that beckoned to me still from Melody's hospital room, my work suffered but at least I was there. Max had some valid points and in the days that followed our confrontation I had no choice but to address them and attempt my return to society.

In my down time I found my mind occupied with certain aspects of the discussion he and I had. I had been so overcome by some emotion that I had prior to that night been unaware of...or at least unable to articulate. My parents had tried to convince me it was depression or anxiety but neither of those felt right. Maybe that is part of depression and anxiety, the inability to distinguish when you have taken on one or both of those states, but it just didn't feel like those titles fit. God knows I had every reason to be depressed, the woman I was planning on marrying in a number of months had been rendered comatose. God knows I had every reason to be anxious too, I had spent countless hours sitting at the bedside of that same comatose woman, watching and waiting for any signs of improvement. Either way, those were not me...I was neither depressed nor anxiety-ridden...or at least if I was those things they took a backseat to a much more powerful sense, and that was guilt.

When I wasn't at work I did my best to not stay with Melody for more time than would have been considered healthy. I would visit every day and sit there in our silence together until another family member would show up. We would all acknowledge each other and carry on whatever conversations we found to be comfortable. I had tried to become more sensitive to when others may have needed time alone with her, and whenever I could, I would go back to my apartment and let them go through whatever process they needed to go through.

It was at my apartment that things were the worst. Prior to the accident Melody stayed over so often that she had her own toothbrush and drawer. She had mostly designed (with my mother) the decor of my apartment and it reeked of her. Color choices of furniture to locations of shelving, all were from her mind, having already planned to spend most of her nights there anyway. Pictures of us with ours and each other's families adorned nightstands and desks and walls. Throw pillows smelled of relaxation oils that she would mist in order to make guests feel more at home, at my home.

I would lock the door and click on the TV and surf channels to try and unwind. Watching any program for the full 30 minutes never helped. I would watch and my mind would wander and always find itself wishing that I was still sitting in that room with her, watching and waiting. I had to change the channel every few seconds to keep my mind occupied with 'what am I seeing' or 'who is that,' and as soon as I figured it out, it was on to the next station.

There were times, still, that even when flipping through the channels that my mind would take over and fill me with terrible thoughts and horrible feelings.

Mostly I wondered how she was doing. I would wonder if there were any changes or if the nurses made sure she was in a comfortable position, if such a thing existed, after cleaning her or moving her around. I would wonder what she was thinking or dreaming or feeling. Often times though, my mind would go back to the night of my argument with Max. Max had agreed that he would face his parents about his feelings toward their post-tragedy behavior and that I would at least try to return to work.

Night would come and I would lay in bed, praying that my mind could shut off and leave me with at least a few hours of restful sleep so that I could continue my charade the next day. Rarely my pleas were successful. On the nights that I was stuck sifting through the turmoil of my mind I would return to the thoughts that colluded against me during that fight with Max. I would be struck with the realization that it was guilt that was preventing me from sleeping, or from being able to make it through the day without a breakdown. It was guilt over Melody's scars, Melody's coma, Melody's silence that haunted me. Guilt that could not be atoned for.

As the weeks since that night had passed, I had conceived a long list of ways in which I could attempt to right the wrong that had befallen her. Knowing that I was unable to wake her from her sleep, I began devising physical torments to force upon myself in the hopes that some-day I would feel that I had paid my debt. The ones whom I had wronged, Melody and her family, expected nothing from me and held me to no account for what happened, so no amount of money or self-flagellation would be expected and no amount would be enough. The guilt was my own and I was able to recognize that, but that did not change the fact that still it existed, and if I ever hoped to rid myself of it, something had to be done.

Work had finished on a Friday and I went back to the apartment instead of my usual afternoon visit to the hospital. I had a new and frightened resolve about what was to come next. I gathered up the items that I would need to begin my process of atonement, hoping that this would in fact help alleviate my guilt. Looking down at the pile of otherwise harmless items, I knew what I was about to do was wrong and I knew that there would not be a single person in my life that would understand what I felt I needed to do, but the feeling of loneliness that accompanies those types of realizations had already become too famil-iar and therefore could not stop me.

There was one item I did not have. It was a simple item for pur-chase at the closest corner drugstore, but I believed that it would have been more symbolic for me to go and take it from the hospital. I ate a small dinner and got in the car to go see her. I needed to explain to her what I was going to do and why it needed to be done. I knew that if she was awake, she, like everyone else, would condemn what I was doing, but if she was awake I wouldn't be doing this.

Her parents were there. I stood just inside the doorway to her room as they sat next to her bed, talking to her, reassuring her, fighting to reassure themselves. They did not cry, they did not sound shaky or disturbed, they, like the rest of us, had become acclimated to Melody's condition. They turned as they stood to leave.

"Sam," her mother said with a smile that she surely would not have if she knew what I was about to do, "How are you?"

"Hi," we hugged, then I hugged her father, "I'm about the same, how are you guys? How's Max?"

"Everyone's alright. Max told us about your time together the other week. You know if you ever need to talk to somebody we are always there for you."

"Thank you, you know that I'm the same way, if you guys or Max need anything, I'm always around."

"We do, Hun, but we worry about you."

"I do too."

They both took those last words as I had hoped but not as I had intended. They understood those words "I do too" to mean that I worry about them as well, but I didn't. They had each other and they had Max, I worried about myself.

We hugged again and they made their way home, leaving me in the room alone with Melody and a sun that was beginning to slowly set in the distance. I sat on one the side of the bed and looked down at the woman I wanted to marry and spoke with her for the first time in a while, breaking from our usual routine of connected silence.

"Hey Mel. Listen, I know that I haven't really said much lately...I've been trying to be strong for you while you've been gone, and it's hard to talk to you when there's nothing for you to say ya know? Anyway, I know you know that I've been here through all of this, and I've been trying hard to keep going and be the same me that I've always been but it's been so hard. I don't think that any of us are the same anymore, I think this has changed all of us. It's my fault, all of it...and no one will accept that."

I sat there in silence, knowing there would be no response but pausing long enough for her to have replied.

"I feel so incredibly guilty for all of it, ya know? And it doesn't get easier, it doesn't get better, every day it just...weighs more. Because of what happened, because I parked us there, because I got out of the car, here you are, stuck in this bed and here I am...drowning. I see your folks or I see Max and I'm ashamed. I feel like it's not just your life but their lives that have been taken too. I wake up every day and I try to remember that you are still alive and here with us, but I don't feel you when we talk...when I talk...you aren't here...you are somewhere that I can't be...I am always...outside of you. Where you are, the closest I can get is when I don't talk...when we just exists together...and even then I don't know if you can hear me."

Silent again, as if that space were being filled with what she might have said. I stared down at the scars on her face, saw the burns on her arms; studied again the wounds inflicted upon her.

"What I need...and I know how selfish this is to ask...like I haven't demanded enough already...but what I need is understanding. These things that are about to happen, they're controlled and hopefully no one will have to find out, but if they do...I know they won't...no one will get it...so I'm asking you to at least try to understand that what I'm about to do I am doing so that I can try to understand you and what you are going through. I'm doing this so that we can change together and I'm doing this in the hopes that this guilt won't weigh so damn much...so please...be patient with me...try to be understanding. Baby I love you so much and I can't even begin to tell you how much I miss you. Where ever you are, whatever you're doing, know those things, and know that I can't wait to kiss you and hold you again and tell you that you are everything to me.

I fought back the tears that came with those final sentiments and bent down to kiss her forehead. This time there were no skipped beats on the heart monitor, no signals that she had heard me or was there...just silence...and that was all I needed.

I told her that I'd be back the next day to tell her about everything, that I wouldn't keep anything from her. I told her I loved her and then I left the room. I began down the hallway toward the elevator as usual, but this time I made a stop into one of the medical supply closets and grabbed some gauze before continuing home.

I returned home after visiting Melody. She was silent again and again so was I. I told her how things had been over the last few days. I told her what I had been doing, and I told her that it was helping a little with the guilt, though it certainly wasn't a part of my day that I looked forward to. My nightly routine was changing into more of a ritual and one that became more horrifying as it became more common-place.

I locked the door behind me and went into my kitchen to start sup-per. My meals were pretty basic now, mostly soft foods like applesauce or pureed vegetables, things with some nutritional value if not caloric. On occasion I would cook up a steak to pamper myself and to make sure my teeth were still functional. I had lost some weight but was unsure how much at that point.

I slurped down my dinner and sat on my couch in front of the tel-evision. Since the guilt had slightly subsided and since the next part of my night required a good amount of focus, I had found that I was able to now make it through an entire half-hour program. Whenever possi-ble I preferred to watch sitcoms and the like. It was a rare occasion in which I would find myself smiling or laughing along with the television audience, but something about the sound of their laughter, the laughter of complete strangers I found comforting.

After the show ended I pulled toward the couch a small ottoman, one that you could find at a department store for not much money; one that had a removable top and could double as a small storage area for photos or movies or otherwise displaced items. I removed the top of the ottoman and began to dig out the items required for the night. In a different context these items were mundane or otherwise unremarkable, mostly household trinkets and a few of the items you may or may not have.

I arranged them in the order in which they were to be used, and separated into two categories, a phase 1 and phase 2 so to speak.

Phase 1 began as I removed both my shirt and undershirt, the latter sticking to the bandages from the previous night. I removed the dress-ings and cleaned the areas with a cotton ball and some rubbing alcohol, preparing them for this night's task. I then picked up the straightened out metal clothes hanger that I had been using. I examined the tip which I had sharpened to ensure the point had been retained since the night before. I began to coil the non-sharpened end around my right hand to prevent me from dropping it. After rubbing some alcohol on the sharp end of the hanger, I grabbed my lighter and began to heat the tip until it glowed.

After watching the dull brass tone turn to a red then white-hot hue, my eyes fixated on it for only a moment, hesitating as I always did out of fear and weakness before plunging it into my ribcage, an inch below and to the right of my left nipple, exactly where Melody's new scar was.

My eyes shut tight and my teeth clenched as I forced the makeshift utensil just below the skin. The pain continued to sear into my flesh, this had not become any easier than the night I first started.

I let out a short cry that stifled itself in midair, disappearing as quickly as the laughter had from the TV. The familiar smell of burning skin returned to my nostrils. I had forgotten to turn on the ceiling fan. My mind tried to focus on Melody to remind myself that she experienced all of the pain at once that I had inflicted on myself over the course of several days. I moved the blade slightly downward at a 45 degree angle, a mirror image of hers, tearing and burning the skin and whatever tissues it would skim across.

Tears exploded from my face as the excruciating agony continued, neither the pain nor the heat would dissipate until after the implement was removed, I had learned that by now. I could slice no longer, the pain had become too much and I removed the lance from my side, applying pressure with a washcloth. I sucked in air through quivering lips as I tried to return my mind to the present and away from the searing torture and the memories of the wreck. I turned my face up to the ceiling, calming myself by staring at the design marbled into the structure, looking for shapes as if staring at clouds.

After a few minute's time I was able to lower my head, my mind calm and my breathing steady. My eyes shut with memories of her, memories of Melody, this time from when we were children. It happened like this every night. I would wound myself and then be flooded with happy memories of our childhood, my body's compensation mechanism for pain I suppose. I felt sadness beyond sadness and emptiness beyond emptiness. My eyes began to flood and tears again fell from my face. I sat there on my couch starting at the items I kept hidden in that ottoman, afraid of them but happy that they were there to help me with my guilt. My chin quivered as I fought back tears and reminded myself that it was now time to continue.

I cleaned the sharpened tip of the hanger again with alcohol and again spent a minute or so heating it as before; my side still throbbing and oozing liquids both red and clear. This second scar would not come from scraping or tearing, this one would be a burnt onto my flesh, same as hers. I applied the tool the front of my right bicep, just above the crease of the elbow. The burns never hurt quite as bad as the gouges but were still very painful and undesirable. I let out my breath slowly through my nostrils as I removed the hanger, reheated and reapplied several times over the course of 5 or so minutes. Once finished, I cleaned both wounds, covered the gash in my side with bandages or gauze, the burn I would cool with aloe or a cold compress.

I sat there covered in my thoughts, understanding what it is I had just subjected myself to and how completely and wholly unhealthy it was. Maybe it was guilt from self-mutilation that replaced the guilt from the wreck, or maybe scarring my body in the way that she had been scarred was actually beginning to make me feel closer to her, either way, I felt better at that moment than I had most of the day.

I sat there still and silent, preparing myself for Phase 2 of my nightly duties. From my ottoman I retrieved two items, ipecac and Ny-Time sleep syrup. I got up and walked into my bathroom, mentally rehearsing the upcoming events.

I figured that the 45 minutes I allowed myself between eating a very basic dinner and now would be plenty in order for my body to get at least some nutrition. I stood in front of the mirror and looked at my arm and at my bandaged side. I walked over and knelt down in front of my toilet. With eyes shut in anticipation I took my swig of ipecac and waiting the few brief moments it took before the effects were felt.

I felt the churning and squeezing in my stomach and began to vomit up the contents therein. I heaved until everything was gone and my stomach housed only bile. I waited for several minutes before attempting to stand. During the expulsion of dinner my head would become dizzy, my eyes would blur, my face would become red with forceful stress, I needed to make sure that all of the substance had been removed before attempting to stand and return to my mirror.

Vomiting was never part of what Melody went through, at least not that I could recall, but emptying my stomach before taking the NyTime syrup helped me sleep deeply and uninterrupted. Granted it was not a coma, but it was as close to it as I could induce on my own.

I swallowed the syrup, brushed my teeth and went to bed. I had an alarm set to go off early enough so that I was able to shower-away the funk from the NyTime medicine and get ready to start the next day, a perpetual repeat of the day before. I lay in bed with my eyes closed, praying that the nightmares that visited me on occasion would not be there tonight.

I had been lucky in the fact that there had only been a few run-ins or close calls with family at the hospital. I think one of the biggest indicators as to whether or not something is a good idea is by the number of people you are okay with telling versus the number of people you try to keep it from. In my case, I had been mutilating myself for nearly a month and the scars were nearly complete, and they were by far my most closely-guarded secret. I could tell no one except the woman lying in the hospital bed, but then again I never tried to make the argument that what I had been doing was a healthy practice. The changes in my appearance were becoming more and more noticeable. I could hardly go an entire day without someone asking me if I was feeling alright. I had dropped a considerable amount of weight.

I had been at the hospital for a few hours by the time my parents had showed up. They gently knocked on the threshold to the room. I turned around to see the smile fade from my mother's face. I stood to face them and as I approached, her grimace turned to tears.

"My God, Sam...What have you done to yourself?"

Believing that there was no way for either of them to know about what was going on every night within the walls of my apartment, I feigned ignorance.

"What are you talking about, Ma?"

"Sammy you look like hell."

"Alright...well...good to see you too." Sarcasm was all I had left.

"Sammy I mean it, what's going on?"

"Mom...I'm fine." I leaned in to hug her, the first hug I had had in a long time. I had not planned on my side hurting as much as it did and I let out a whimper that she either didn't hear or pretended not to hear.

I looked over at my dad, his face wrought with concern as well.

"Sam," he started before I interrupted.

"Dad, if this isn't you telling me that it's good to see me...please just don't."

He took a moment, fighting to replace worry with anything else he could think of.

"It's good to see you, boy."

We walked over to the side of Melody's bed and looked down at her. We stood there silent for a few minutes, my parents leaning against each other, my father's arm around my mother; her hand on my shoulder.

"She hasn't changed much in the last few weeks, but I'm hopeful."

"Good."

"We all are, dear."

"Yeah...thanks for coming to see her."

"You know son, we came to see you too. It feels like it's been forever since we have seen or heard from you. What have you been doing? HOW have you been doing?"

I turned to look my father in the eye. I tried to so hard to think of anything that would not rouse suspicion in him.

"I've been OK. It hasn't been easy going back to work. Most of the time my mind is here in this room but I get through my days-"

-"And what are you doing with your free time? I know you aren't here always because we have come by to see you and you're not here."

"Well, Mom...I spend a lot of time at home. I try to relax and keep my mind occupied...TV and stuff."

"I hope you're not drinking or taking drugs."

I smiled a little at my mother's concern and verbiage.

"No Ma, I'm not doing any drugs."

"Good. Well, you know you can always come by and see us whenever you want."

"I know. I've needed some time to myself to work through things."

"Well you know you don't have to do that on your own."

"Yeah."

"Well dear I think we should head out, give Sam some more time with his bride-to-be."

"Thanks. I'll come by sometime soon."

"Please do, Sam. We miss you a lot."

"Miss you too, dad."

My father put his hand around my neck and pulled me in and kissed my forehead. It was a sweet gesture and I was relieved that he didn't go for a hug. My mother on the other hand felt the need to wrap me in her arms and squeeze. I think she was trying to make a point about my weight loss.

They both went over to Melody, I stayed where I was. Dad bent down to kiss her on the forehead in the same way he had done to me moments before. Mom was still a little bit timid around her body and opted to smile as my father stood back up. They smiled at her and then at me before leaving the room.

One development regarding everyone's acceptance of Melody's coma was that they had let go of the idea of an 'obligatory visit.' My folks, hers, no one came just to say they spent time with her that day. Sure her parents did come by at least once a day, usually in the evenings after work or occasionally during their lunches, but the feeling of guilt that initially accompanied anyone leaving the room went away. No one watched the clock to make sure they had spent an adequate amount of time next to her, they came and went as they needed to. When people came to visit, it was because they wanted to see her; people had begun to make their peace with the stability of her condition, despite its horrific circumstances.

Maybe that's just how people work; part of the misery that comes with tragedy is simply the change. Once we learn how to live our lives with that change, whether someone dies or gets a divorce or falls into a coma that is when we begin to heal. At this point philosophy and insight like that meant nothing to me and had no bearing on the course I had set in motion. My mind had begun to weaken in the same fashion as my body. I was dreaming every night and rarely were they dreams that were comforting or warm; dreams of nightmares that would be unbroken thanks to the deep sleep insured by the NyTime medicine.

I returned to my chair next to Melody and as we sat in our silence. I had explained my nightly routine to Melody shortly after I had started. I had explained to her that I was doing all of this so that I could better understand the pain that she must've experienced before it sent her into her coma.

My current dilemma was that the wounds I had been carving into my body were nearly complete and I wasn't sure what would happen once they were. I had wanted them to resemble hers as closely as possible, and considering the two separate natures of how they were imposed, I would say they were pretty damn close.

My fear right then was that when the wounds were finished the guilt that their infliction had helped reduce would return. After the current scars were complete, the only one I would be without would be one to match the one on Melody's face and I knew I would be unable to duplicate that one without someone trying to stop me. It was a large enough scar that there was no way I could do it all in one night. I had become well-practiced at experiencing my flesh tearing, but this would be one thing too many.

We sat there in silence as I explained it all to her. I still couldn't stand talking to her, knowing that there was no way she could respond, so I told her everything I had been doing, through thought. I explained my fear of the guilt coming back even stronger, and I told her that I would try to think of some other way to make things right. I told her I loved her and that I missed her. I told her I was sorry for hurting myself and that I was sure it was not something she would have approved of, but that it was something I needed, and I acknowledged my selfishness. Before leaving I asked her through my thoughts to come visit me in one of my dreams to make them brighter and to let me know that she was OK.

It was 5 days after that night that she did just that; it was the night that I had finished the final scar on the inside of my right thigh. I had bandaged up my leg and drank my nightly fluids and went to bed. She had come to me that night, telling me that she missed me and that didn't want me to have to feel any pain and that she didn't feel any. It was her voice, I didn't see her but I could hear her clearly. She told me that she loved me and that she would be there for me from now on, whenever I needed her, all I had to do was sleep. If there was any more to that dream I do not remember it and when I woke up I began to cry; having heard her voice for the first time in months only to have it be a dream proved to be more than I could bear. After I finished crying I put on a brave face and went to work, telling myself the whole thing was a dream and nothing more, it was not until that evening that I began to believe otherwise.

That day had been nothing out of the ordinary save for the fact that I knew I would not be cutting into or burning my skin that night, a fact that left me both relieved and fearful. The question that repeatedly had been whispered into my ear from nothingness was whether or not the guilt that mutilating helped to keep at bay would return, and if so, to what degree.

I had decided during my lunch hour that I would fix myself a worthwhile dinner that night and then go to see Melody during the time that I would have normally devoted to scar-duplication. I figured that the best way to keep the beast away was to re-dedicate my time to being by her side until I knew what to do next.

In so far as the rest of the day was concerned, things were normal. I put in my time at the office and headed home. The familiar sound of the deadbolt engaging filled me initially with dread. I had apparently programmed a Pavlovian response to the door lock and torture. It was a quick realization but one that would take more than just a few nights to get passed. I fixed myself a steak and a potato and sat in front of the television. I figured that sitting in front of the TV would be the first real test regarding guilt's response to my having finished my self-imposed trial. If I could make it through a show for the full 30 minutes without having to channel surf in order to keep my mind occupied, well...that would be a good start.

I drown my steak with sauce and decided which show to watch, trying fully to immerse myself in the delights of one or both items. Much to my surprise I felt fine. I had filled my stomach with food that was destined to fully digest, and I had lost myself to the ongoing drama of a reality show about fat folks competing to see who can lose the most weight. I was happy for myself, happy for the contestants in the TV, and for the first time since the ordeal had started, excited to go see Melody.

It was probably because of her voice, that beautiful voice that came to me in my dream last night and reassured me that she was without pain and that I needn't suffer it for her, but I had a renewed sense of comfort. I believed the words she said to me last night, and I believed that she was somewhere away from me but that she would find a way to return to me as soon as she could.

An Imperfect Fortress

I left my place and headed toward the hospital, smiling a smile that had not been on my face for a very long time. My mind was never foolish enough to let my happiness go unchecked. I sorted through thoughts and emotions on that drive, fighting the instinct to believe in something as good as that dream, trying to reason my way out of the relief that I felt in those moments. I fought against my mind, trying to so hard to believe that she did come to me in that dream. I knew how ridiculous that idea was, but it was the closest thing to a happy thought that I had to cling to in quite a while, and I wasn't about to let it be torn away from me.

I made it to the hospital and to her bedside. I sat there and I looked down at her, a smile still spread across my face, as if to say to her "I got your message."

I sat in silence as I always did, speaking to her through thought. In my thoughts I thanked her for visiting me and giving me the reassurance I so badly needed. I told her again that the scars were finished, the trial successfully completed. I told her I feared the guilt would return, but that if it did I would find a way to deal with it. I told her that even if that guilt never returned there was still so much of it left to deal with. I remember these next moments with great clarity:

I was watching her, my eyes scanning her beautiful face, telling her that I couldn't wait to fall asleep so that I could hear her voice again. It was right in the middle of my next thought as I reached and grabbed her hand, "I wish you would open yo-"

Her eyes shot open.

I sat there in shock, staring at her glossy eyes, unable to move, unsure as to whether or not this was reality or if this was an illusion brought about by an exhausted mind.

"doctor." I could barely get the word out.

"DOCTOR!!!" The word spilling out of me as loudly as any word ever had as I backed toward the doorway, afraid to take my sight off of her unblinking eyes.

"HELP...ANYBODY!!!" Two members of the nurse staff came running in, one to each side of Melody, each scanning the monitors and print-outs of any change in Melody's outputs. The nurse to Melody's left ran out of the room and returned after a short time with a doctor. His first question very calmly stated:

"What happened?"

I stammered, "I dunno, I...I...I was just talking to her. Her eyes....they shot open...can she see?

The doctor shined a light into her eyes, obviously looking for any papillary response, what he saw or did not see I do not know. He put the light back into the breast pocket of his scrubs and turned to look through the read-outs on the machines as the nurses had. I stood in my corner, still not knowing if what I was seeing was actually happening, praying that this was real and more importantly, that this meant that she was coming back to me. Minutes passed like hours as everyone coming in and going out of the room moved with a rush in the step. I was helpless and useless, I served no purpose at that point, I was the only body in that room that didn't need to be there, but I knew I was the one person that needed to be there the most. I don't know who would have called her parents or after how long since her eyes had opened that they were called, but there they were, and time resumed its regular pace.

I broke my stare from Melody as I heard her father's voice.

"Is she awake?"

Dr. and Mrs. Black entered the room in a frenzy, completely by-passing me in my corner to see Melody's open eyes. They exchanged excited and hopeful glances to each other and then back down to their daughter. After a several minutes they turned and found me, fearful that if I had imagined all of this that I had been the one to drag them in to my hallucination.

"Son," Emmett said with calm in his voice, "come here."

I made my way slowly to his side, unsure of what to do.

"Tell me everything," he grabbed my shoulders tightly and stared me in the eye.

"I was sitting here, next to her..." my eyes broke his gaze as they danced around trying to remember every minute detail of the moment.

"Sam," he fought to bring my focus back to him, "what happened?"

"I grabbed her hand and was talking to her, telling her..." I stopped short of telling him I asked her to open her eyes. I knew that if I had told him the truth about that moment, about that one detail, it would seem too crazy and they would think that I was losing my mind, or that they would believe me and ask me to tell her to wake up...something I was too scared to do.

"Telling her what, Sam?" His grip tightening through angst.

"I miss her, I was telling her I how much I miss her and her eyes looked up at me."

Her dad's stare broke from my eyes as he turned to his wife, my would-be mother-in-law and then to the doctor, still trying to get a read on what exactly was happening.

"What do we do?" Emmett asked.

The doctor looked up at him from his work,

"Nothing right now, just be patient and I'll let you know as soon as I do."

We waited the next while as the nurses would leave and return, as would the doctor. Sometimes there would be extra bodies in the room; nurses that we were not familiar with or doctors that were curious or thought that they may be able to better assess the situation or provide some insight as to what was going on. None were able to and before any of us had realized, it was 2 in the morning. I asked Melody's dad if we should call Max, at that point so much time had passed and Melody's eyes had begun to sink back behind their lids. I had thought that maybe bringing Max in would be enough to bring about some sort of response from her if she could muster any more.

No. I don't think we should tell Max about this."

"What, like...at all?"

"Yeah, not until we know more."

With those words the doctor returned to the room and asked us to sit. Melody's mom was already seated next to me and her dad decided he felt better standing. The doctor pulled up a rolling stool and told us that while her eyes had opened there had been no significant change in her readouts, and that more than likely her eyes had opened as more of a physical reaction to some stimulus as opposed to any sort of development or sign that she may be coming out of her condition.

We all had our questions for him.

"What does this mean going forward?" or "Will this happen again?"

His answers were about as middle-of-the-road as any I had ever heard.

"We don't know for certain what will happen in the upcoming hours/days/weeks or months." or "There's no way of knowing if this will happen again," but the gist of the discussion was that Melody's eyes opening could be something or could be nothing.

Melody's parents both succumb to tearful emotions: sadness, anger, fear. I was left with a completely different impression from the experience, but then again I was the only one that actually knew the full truth of what had happened that night. The truth was that I connected to her. I told her to open her eyes and she did. Yes it scared the hell out of me and it got a lot of people worked up in both hopeful and dreadful ways, but still...it was something...and I had had my fill of nothing lately.

The doctor asked if there was anything else we needed from him. Emmett told him we just need to be kept up to date of any changes.

"Of course," the doctor replied in a very practiced tone of sympathy.

I told them that I wanted to go ahead and stay the rest of the night by her side, the doctor said that would be OK and he would have a pillow and blanket sent in. I thanked him and he left the room. Emmett expressed some concern that the stress of the night would take a toll and that I should go home to rest in a bed instead of sitting in a chair hoping for something to happen again. I told him I appreciated the concern and let him know that I wasn't going to be able to sleep after what had happened and that I'd rather be awake here than awake in an otherwise empty apartment.

The three of us ended the night by exchanging hugs which still required a good amount of focus to keep my face from registering the pain from my new scars. I told them I was sorry that her eyes opening didn't come to mean anything more than it did. No one wanted Melody to snap out of this coma more than I did, but despite the doctor's words to us, I still believed something was happening. I returned to Melody's side slowly, almost as if I expected her eyes to dart open again and make me piss myself. I sat in the chair, and with her eyes closed again and the room empty of everyone except us, it was hard not to think that the whole episode never happened at all. I grabbed her hand and returned to sending her my thoughts. I thanked her for letting me see into her beautiful eyes, and I told her that I was going to be right there for the rest of the night in case she needed me.

Melody's eyes impacted each of us differently in the days follow-ing the event. Her father seemed more on edge and coped with the stress of his new level of uncertainty by researching as much as he could about comas...which was difficult I imagine as he had poured through every bit of material he could after the wreck had happened. After a week or so we had ran into each other at the hospital, he ex-plained to me that its very rare for anyone in a coma to just wake up like they do in the movies. He explained that more often than not pa-tients that wake up have no idea what is going on or where they are and have no realization that they were ever in a coma.

"Most of the time they can't even speak for a little while," he ex-plained.

He ended that talk with me by reassuring me that he still believed that Melody opening her eyes was significant and that he thought it was just the next step in her progressing toward recovery. I agreed with him and forced as much of a smile at him as I could stand.

He had seen through the facade of my smile and saw that I had been struggling ever since that night. He asked me what was going on with me and what had I been going through. My answers were as mid-dle-of-the-road as the doctors had been that night. I told him I doing 'Ok...all things considered." I told him that it was still a daily struggle but that I had found a decent balance with work and home. But the truth was much different.

The truth was that the guilt had returned in full force and I had no idea now how to deal with it. After Melody had opened her eyes I was so sure that it was because of me, because I had asked her to, because we were truly connected for the first time since the tragedy. In the nights after that I returned to my usual schedule of work, dinner, hos-pital, sleep, repeat. I had been so proud of myself after having finished my self-mutilation and that thanks to my penance I was able to return to some semblance of normalcy. I was beside myself with excitement and something close to hope when she opened her eyes, but after that night, nothing changed. Like I said, I went back to my schedule having gained nothing and now I was beginning to think that those feelings of hope and excitement were illusions, another means for my mind to compensate for the sadness.

Melody stopped visiting in my dreams, her voice no longer in my ears as my eyes would open to each new day. I was able to fall asleep without the aid of any medicine, but that sleep was empty, void of beautiful voices and void of nightmares and monsters. The silence of my dreams eventually became the reason I lost sleep. I had become so invested in the idea of Melody being there every time I had closed my eyes that when it stopped, I no longer wanted sleep at all.

My folks had called me to make good on that promise I had given them for dinner. I made plans to go over and eat with them in the latter part of the week and by the day of, I had actually found myself somewhere close to excited to see them. I never dreaded going home for visits, I love my family very much, I just hadn't been excited about much since the wreck, and finding that feeling in me was a pleasant surprise.

I opened the door to my parent's house greeted by the smell of roast and the chatter of people that seemed to emanate from the kitchen area. I walked down the hall and turned to find my folks as well as Max and Dr. and Mrs. Black.

"Sam!" Max came over and gave me a hug.

"Hey Max," I said as we finished our man-embrace.

"I didn't know everyone was going to be here."

"We decided to have everyone over earlier this afternoon, kind of a last-minute decision," my dad let me know as he held a beer up to his lips.

"Ahh...well...good to see everyone," I said through a smile.

Emmitt stayed near my dad, talking work and who knows what else, Max's mother came over and hugged me as well.

"It's so good to see you outside of the hospital, dear."

I smiled and nodded to her, knowing what she meant but curious at how she had decided to form that sentence.

"Mom, is there anything I can help with?"

"No, go sit, the food will be out in a minute."

I left the kitchen with Max following right behind me. We sat next to each other at the table; the same spots we had sat in our entire lives. I asked him what he had been up to since not returning to school; he told me about some job that he had found and that he hated it and already knew he would go back to school when the next semester starts in January. He asked me questions about work and asked what I had been up to the past month since we had last seen each other. I didn't have much of a response other than things were fine, I wasn't about to spill the beans about my past cutting and burning ritual, so I left things at that.

The night went on and everything was pleasant. To be honest it was the first time that I felt comfortable using that word in the post-wreck world, everything was just...pleasant. We all had a good meal and the conversation wasn't forced, there were no long, painful or awkward silences, just us as being as close to a family as we could with one member not there.

Max and I enjoyed a few drinks together after dinner, playing card games with everyone as we had the night of the accident, and at some point in the night each of us could say we had a sincere laugh. I decided to stay the night in my old room at my parent's house since I had been drinking; hoping that maybe a night in a house with other bodies in it may even be therapeutic.

I remember lying in bed, staring up at the ceiling, beginning to realize that staying there may have been a mistake. Though the night had gone well and I had had my first experience in which I wasn't on the verge of tears at every moment, my mind would not turn off. Still with every inch of my room, every fiber in my bed I could remember some beautiful and now painful memory of Melody. I would turn to my side and see the TV against my wall and remember New Year's Night. I would turn to face my window and have a perfect view into her old room and remember the night we got each other off by watching one another. Memories that I had fought so hard to bury for the time being came screaming to the forefront of my mind and I was unable to prevent each new moment from being overtaken with emotion.

I sat up in bed, rubbing my tired eyes and placed my feet squarely on the ground. I found my footing and headed to the bathroom. I hunkered over the sink, cold water filling my cupped hands before splashing over my face. I did this a few times. It was while I was dabbing my face dry with a towel that I remembered the NyTime medicine that was always kept behind the mirror. I hoped that the contents of the nearly emptied bottle would be my salvation. I removed the cap and placed the mouth of the bottle to my lips and began to drink every drop that would roll out; after that I filled the bottle with water and drank the remnants before returning to bed. It was not long before my eyes grew heavy and I drifted off to a beautifully deep and medicated sleep.

I slept wonderfully and without being disturbed until late the following morning. I woke up to light-filled room and for the first time in a while, I could hear Melody's voice echoing again in my ears.

That next week was dedicated to maintaining my sanity. For the first time in a while, I had heard her voice again, and it stayed with me throughout my days. You ever have a dream that impacts your day? Maybe you have a dream where someone dies and for the rest of the day you can't help but carry that feeling of sadness or melancholy around with you? That is about as close of an analogy as I can come up with for what I was going through. The difference really is that I had resumed my struggle with believing that maybe this was more than just a dream...that it really was her. She first spoke to me when I finished my scars...she opened her eyes shortly after at my request...I couldn't let those sorts of things rest at coincidence. Yes she had maintained radio silence for the past two weeks, but now she was back, and all I needed to do was figure out why.

I left my parents' house after lunch that day and went to see Melody in the hospital, thinking maybe something had changed and her words to me last night had been a call, asking me to come and see her. I stayed with her for a few hours in our silence, telling her that I heard her last night and that if there was anything she needed or wanted, all she ever had to do was tell me. There was no response from her, no movement, no eyes opening, no words, nothing. I wasn't surprised, I wasn't let down, I just had to remind myself that when I spoke to her like that, through my thoughts, it was never meant to be a conversation, just a reassurance to her.

Her parents showed up around 5 o'clock that evening to see their daughter. I talked to them for a few minutes about nothing important and then said my goodbyes for the evening to everyone. I went back to my place and decided to watch some television, eat some dinner and try to get the feeling that had followed me around all day to leave. I cooked a small meat-and-potatoes type of meal and leaned over in front of the fridge to get a beer. It was the moment that the beer hit my lips that I realized that that was what made last night different: I had been drinking.

My heart and mind were at odds with each other, warring about the implications of such a thought. If Melody only came to me when I drink, then surely that would mean that I'm some sort of crazy and the whole thing was brought about by booze, a cheap parlor trick that carried with it no significant meaning at all. My heart, the part of me that wanted to believe more than anything that Melody could communicate with me, refused to believe that something so tawdry would be responsible for her vocal night time visits. There was only one way to find out...so I drank, and drank...and then for good measure I drank more.

I passed out on the couch that night, my dinner half-eaten and the television still on. It was late Sunday morning before my eyes cracked open, my head splitting from the sun bleeding into my apartment and the sound of the laughter screaming from the TV. I woke up with having not heard from Melody. Again, different reactions to the lack of a visit were happening inside of me. My mind was angry that I had been wrong in my assumption of it being alcohol that caused of Melody to visit. My heart however was thrilled to know that I had been wrong, alcohol had nothing to do with those visits, and the possibility that she was in fact trying to reach me was still very much alive...even if I was no closer to understanding the pattern in which she chose to come to me.

I nursed my hangover with some Tabasco and an over-easy egg on toast, orange juice with a bit of vodka. My headache would not go away with any amount of medication or water, my body's very angry way of telling me I was an idiot for last night's 'experiment.' I spent the day trying to keep my mind and body occupied. I went to visit her after dinner, again there were no developments. In our silence I confessed my drinking theory to her, secretly a little happy that she would not be able to respond with the laughter and consternation that would have undoubtedly come my way. I sat there with her limp hand in mine, continuing to watch and hope for anything only to be let down again. I kissed her and went home.

Night crept into my apartment and wrapped me in its cold arms as I sat alone on my couch. My television was on but I wasn't watching it, I was staring past it, stuck in my own mind and unable to shake an awful sadness that had burrowed its way into my heart. I had mutilated myself to sate my guilt's hunger, a hunger kept at bay by a thin wall that I knew could not hold forever. I was no closer to understanding anything I had set out to understand and it felt that we were no closer to knowing anything about what Melody was going through or how long things would last.

Thoughts turned into wasted hours of depression and loneliness as I realized I needed to try and sleep. It was getting late and I could tell that my mind would not be able to shut itself off that night, no matter how tired I had become. Before going to bed I found my way to the bathroom and pulled out a fresh bottle of NyTime medicine and began to drink. I undressed and crawled between my sheets, listening closely to the blades of my ceiling-fan cut through the silence that pervaded the dark. It took some time but eventually the medicine began to work its way through my system and I succumbed to a deep sleep. It was that next morning that I finally realized what the catalyst was...a realization that came as my eyes opened and Melody's voice hung in the air.

I started that day as though I had a renewed sense of purpose. I shot out of bed, showered, ate, went to work. I sat at my desk anxiously tapping away at my computer trying to make the hours pass as quickly as I could. I needed to go see Melody, I needed to tell her that I figured out what she was trying to tell me and then I had to test it...I needed to put it all to the test before I could fully evaluate my course and plan my next move.

Usually when you need a day to fly by it drags, this day was different. I needed things to hurry along, I needed the hour hand to move as quickly as it could...and that day it seemed happy to oblige. 5 o'clock came and I left work and went straight to the hospital. I was there alone for half an hour before any other family showed up. I sat next to Melody as I always did and grabbed her had as I always did. I sat there and sent her my thoughts, telling her I was grateful that she came to me last night when I was at the end of my rope. I was thankful to hear her voice and I was excited get back to a place that would allow me to hear it every night until she returned to me.

My folks showed up this time, again about half an hour after I had been there. There was light conversation about how much fun we all had at dinner those few nights ago. I hugged them and left to go to the corner drug store. I bought only 2 of the 7 or so bottles of NyTime, not wanting to appear to the kid behind the register that I was some sort of addict...in fact unsure as to whether or not any one person would be allowed to purchase that much of the stuff without sending up any red flags.

I spent my $15 that night on medicine that I was planning to abuse. I certainly didn't see it that way at the time. I didn't stop to think that I was about to ingest a considerable amount of this medicine designed to treat symptoms I did not have. I saw it instead as me being certain that I had a way to hear the voice of the most beautiful woman in the world any night I wanted, a voice that had for too long been silent.

I rushed home and microwaved my dinner; some left overs accompanied by a bottle of beer would cover me for the night. I finished and didn't bother moving the dishes to the sink. I started toward the bathroom, bottle of NyTime in hand, my pace slowing as I fumbled with the outside seal. I found myself in front of my mirror, finally able to remove the wrapping and remove the measuring cup. I began to pour the thick red liquid into the cup to dull out my 2 tablespoons before realizing that the dosage rules didn't really apply to me since I didn't exhibit any of the symptoms it had been designed to fight. I threw the contents of the cup down the back of my throat before drinking two gulps straight from the bottle.

I pulled it from my lips and wiped the excess away with the back of my hand. I put the cap back on and undressed. I went to my bedroom, drew the blinds and shut the curtains in an attempt to make the room as dark as possible, sunset wouldn't come for another hour or so and there was still plenty of natural evening light flooding my west-facing bedroom windows. I looked at the clock and the last thing I remember from that night is seeing 7:24 staring at me as I tried to calculate the number of hours of sleep I could get away with.

I was right, it had been the medicine that brought her voice to me. I spent the next week confirming that suspicion, and without fail, if I drank enough NyTime, I would wake up having felt as though I had just finished hearing Melody's voice. Some mornings I would awaken with full recall of what she had said, some mornings would be less so, but the feeling that came from hearing her each time was just as profound as the nights that I could remember everything.

In a similar way to when I thought it was simply alcohol that would bring her voice to me, my mind and my heart were at war regarding the implication. Yes I understood that in order to pacify my need to hear her voice I had to abuse a substance I was using to self-medicate. My mind understood what I was doing and why it was wrong, but those facts were outweighed by the fact that the end result of that abuse was hearing her and feeling connected to her in a way I had not felt since my last abusive endeavor of self-mutilation.

My heart felt content and utterly shattered every time I would go down that path, but as far as I could see at the time, it was the only path that would make me feel close to her and that was worth so much more than the pain. At first she would tell me simple things: I love you or I miss you...things like that.

After a week or so I started asking her questions as a test. The thought that all of this was imaginary and that the voice I was hearing was simply the memory of her voice coupled with Codeine and a drastic desire to believe something good could happen was never far from my mind. Again, I realized how crazy all of this was and that was exactly why I couldn't tell anyone but again...if you had the chance to speak to or at least hear the voice of someone you love and miss...wouldn't you do the same?

I would sit there next to her during our time together in the hospital, holding her hand and sending her my thoughts as always. My thoughts had shifted from the usual sentiments to asking her what she was feeling or thinking...I would ask her if she was dreaming in there and if she knew I was there...if she knew that all of us were there. I would ask her when she was coming back, but never if she was coming back...I never gave her that option.

There was one night that she came to me, I had dosed and fallen asleep. That next morning I woke up knowing that we had a conversation. She was answering the questions I had asked. She told me that she was fine and didn't feel much. She wasn't dreaming, she was just there...aware that I was there and that her family was there. She was aware of everything. She said she couldn't hear what people were saying but could feel their thoughts and that that was how she knew what was going on.

She heard my thoughts; she felt the thoughts of those who were there for her. She felt sad to cause so much sadness...something I told her to never feel again. She told me that she wished she could come back and tell everyone that things were OK and to apologize for the whole ordeal. I became upset and told her that no one blames her and that it was not her fault. She told me that she knew no one blamed her for any of it, but that she knew no one blamed me either...she was aware of the guilt I felt and tried to convince me it was unnecessary. I acknowledged her feelings toward that 'unnecessary guilt' and reminded her that it was because of that guilt that I was able to talk to her in the first place. I opened my eyes after that, still feeling her speak to me, saying that what would be next would be the hardest, but that we could make it through anything.

In the nights that followed she would only speak to me about the memories that we had...the memories I have mentioned already. Many nights we relived our meeting as children, the trampoline, our first date, the night we first made love, everything except for our engagement. I was thankful for those nights and for those memories, many of which I had stopped thinking about for fear of pain. The pain that came with reliving them in my dreams was made better by the thought that Melody had been experiencing them with me, and as bittersweet as it was, it was perfect.

Our lives together had already been so full of laughter and happiness that it seemed unfair or selfish to want the rest of our lives to continue that way, but when has anyone ever said "Stop, that's enough happiness for one lifetime?"

My nights continued on like this for a month. I would medicate and sleep for 10-12 hours at a time, each night being visited by the love of my life and either hearing her beautiful voice or reliving some great memory or episode of my life with her. We understood exactly what the arrangement was; I would never ask her when she was going to wake up and she would never ask me to relay messages to her family. If she knew when she was going to wake up, she never told and she knew that I would never be able to explain to my family or hers that I was able to communicate with their daughter so long as I was abusing NyTime.

It was at the end of that month that I decided to take a week off of work. My nights had become so important to me that the toll of being awake was beginning to affect me in negative ways. I had become overrun with anxiety, scared that each night would be the last night that she would be there. Anxiety was waiting for me every time I closed my eyes for the night, scared that we would have to relive the night of the accident. I would stare at the phone at my desk during work hours anticipating any sort of call from the hospital or from family...I was becoming unable to cope with those things and decided to take a few days to submerge as fully as I could to my dream world with Melody.

I told my family and hers that I was taking a week off of work to travel and recharge my batteries. I told them all that I needed to have some time to myself and that I would find some nice place that I could drive to and just unplug. I told them I needed to be away from the hospital, away from work, away from everything. I told them I would be back at the end of the week and that we could all catch up on my cathartic experience when I return. No one questioned it; I guess they had all seen the toll that the past 4 months since the wreck had taken on me and not a single person tried to stop me.

I was able to secure 5 days off from work, a full Monday-Friday workweek. That, coupled with the weekends both before and after would give me nine days to sleep. I spent the days leading up to that first Saturday stopping in at various corner stores and gas stations, picking up a bottle of the medicine here and there, succeeding in not triggering any suspicion from the folks behind the counter, though after a while I began to feel that I could buy 17 bottles at once and they wouldn't bat an eye.

Friday came and I watched the clock approach 5 pm. I left work and went to see Melody. I sat with her for an hour, as always holding her hand and thinking my supportive thoughts to her. I explained to her my plan for the next 9 days and how I had stocked up on NyTime and bottles of water and energy bars for the few moments that I would wake up hungry. I told her I hoped that my plan would work and that I couldn't wait to spend that time with her. I kissed her forehead and returned her hand to her side. I left the hospital and headed to surprise my parents at their place.

I walked into the house and could smell warm and welcoming things baking in the kitchen. I entered the kitchen as my mom turned to look at me, shocked that I would show up out of the blue of my own volition. She called for my dad, the puzzled and playful look on her face suggesting that he had something to do with my sudden appearance. He showed up behind me a moment later, grabbing and squeezing my shoulders and asking what I was doing there.

I turned while remaining in the doorway so that he could enter the kitchen and join Mom. He put his arm around her and her oven-mitten-clad hand wrapped around his waist.

"To what do we owe this pleasure?"

I looked down to the tiled kitchen floor and smiled before looking up at them, "Nothing...I just wanted to stop by before I head out."

"We kinda thought you had already left." Dad said.

"I thought about it, but I wanted to come by and see you guys before I take off."

"Well thank you son, when will we see you next?"

"I'll only be gone a week, I'll try to come by next weekend."

"Well don't worry if you are too tired from your trip."

"Shouldn't be...resting up is kind of the whole point."

"Yeah...just...come see us whenever you can, we always love seeing you."

"I know Pop, I love seeing you guys too."

"Mom's baking some cupcakes; you want to stay and have one with us?"

"Of course."

I stayed and spoke with my parents for the better part of an hour. We stayed in the kitchen and remained standing, each of us leaning against one surface or another as the time went by. I hugged and kissed them both and Mom made sure to send me off with a bag-full of cupcakes for the road. I made it to my car and as the door shut I was overcome with emotion and couldn't help but cry in big heaping sobs.

That past hour of pleasantry and conversation took such a toll on me mentally that I collapsed emotionally, as if having run some great distance. It had been such a long time since I had been able to maintain such a convincingly happy charade that the presence of silence and the absence of courtesy overran me entirely.

I gave myself the time needed to belt out the sobs, hoping that no one would notice my car was still parked outside. My attention had been drawn to the lights coming on from the Black household and became afraid that Max would spot my vehicle if he had not done so already. I started the car and headed back to my apartment, knowing that what was to come next would be equal parts sick and therapeutic.

I had said the goodbyes to my folks and to the Black family. They all believed I was leaving town for the week in an attempt to unwind or otherwise 'recharge.' They believed that I would be in some idyllic setting, gathering my thoughts and trying to cope in a more healthy way than I had been. From what I told them I would be sitting on a deck on some body of water, still and contemplative. What I was about to do, in reality, could not be further from the truth.

I had purchased my weeks' worth of NyTime, a crate of bottled water, four boxes full of high-calorie snack bars and black out curtains. I had prepared for myself a week of medicine-induced sleep. I knew that there would be moments, short windows of time in which the medicine would wear off or my body would otherwise reject the notion of sleep. I had hoped that those windows would be as brief as possible and to assist my body in accepting the codeine, I would keep my stomach empty, save for occasional sips of water and bites of those protein bars.

I sat in my apartment, waiting for the first hints of nightfall. My body was so excited that it was difficult to relax. I suppose that is irony isn't it? I was so excited for my week of sleep that I was having difficulty convincing myself I was tired. I skipped dinner that night, wanting my stomach to be as empty as possible so that the NyTime medicine could enter into my system as quickly as it could. It was nearly 8 o'clock in the evening when I found myself unable to contain my nervous excitement any longer. I needed to go to sleep, I needed to see Melody, I needed to feel her and to hear her.

I ripped open the bottle and began to drink. I was able to consume half of the bottle without stopping for breath. I wiped away the excess from my lips and stared at the red stain it had made on the back of my hand. It brought me comfort, a confirmation of sorts that what I had been so excited for would soon be arriving. I drew the black-out curtains and my room was dark. I lay there in anticipation, tossing and turning and waiting for the warm slip of drowsiness to consume me. My eyes fixated on the red light shining from my alarm clock, a device, I had realized, that would not be needed for the next several days. The last thing I remember is unplugging the alarm clock and pulling myself back onto the mattress, it was 8:47. I had not been able to cover myself with blankets before succumbing to the pull of the medicine as it drug me down into a deep sleep.

The first time I had awakened I did not remember seeing or interacting with Melody, but I do remember hearing her voice echoing in my head as it had so many times before. My eyes slowly drew open, there was no light fighting to enter the room from the outline of the curtains. I did not know what time it was and I did not care. I knew I was thirsty beyond belief, and I knew that I needed to go back to sleep. I could feel Melody inside of my head, waiting and pleading for me to return to her. I dropped my arm down the side of my bed, flailing my hand about trying to find one of the many bottles of water I had stashed there. I had succeeded and ripped the cap off and began to sip. My sips quickly turned into full-fledged drinks and then to giant gulps as I tried to quench my thirst. The bottle had emptied into my mouth, I swallowed the last drops of water before throwing the plastic to the ground. The cold of the water had awoken my mind even more and I began to fear that I would be unable to return to sleep. I grabbed the remaining half-empty bottle of NyTime and finished it's contents. I lay there still in the darkness and faded back into the emptiness of my sleep, waiting for her to arrive.

She came to me, whether it was the second or third trip under or the fifth I am not sure. What I am sure of is that she was there. Time meant nothing to me and I had no reality of it. It could have flown by or it could have moved slowly and I would never have known the difference, I had achieved exactly what I had hoped to and that was all that mattered.

There in the darkness and in the void of my dream she stood, beautiful and smiling, happily waiting for my return. I joined her and grabbed her hand as we watched each other, motionless, speechless but entwined in one another. She watched me as I eventually gave way to my questions:

"is this real?"

She continued to stare into me, I could feel her voice without her lips having to move. I understood what she wanted to say, she wanted to tell me that real or not, it felt like we were together and that was all she needed. She knew that all I needed was to feel connected to her, and in that commonality we resonated and enjoyed our love again.

These several days passed in my sleep with conversations, memories, embraces; each interrupted only by brief episodes of consciousness.

I later found that I had been in that bed and in that sleep for 5 days though that bed is not where I woke up.

It was on that fifth day that I had a visitor, someone not expecting to find what they had found, and someone that was trying to do something good for me and in return I gave her the scare of her lifetime. My mother came over shortly after 5 in the afternoon to clean my apartment. She had figured that I would be returning from my vacation in a couple of days and would appreciate coming back to a nice, clean apartment.

She entered my place with the key I had given her when I signed my lease. She had brought with her a pale full of bottle cleansers and her trusty vacuum. Before she could begin to clean a smell caught her by surprise, a stench of urine and bowel, a stench she believed (albeit incorrectly) to come from my bathroom.

She eventually found that the bathroom was not the source of the foul odor and made her way to my bedroom door knowing there was no way anyone or anything could be in there. She later told me that she was filled with fear and that she could feel her body pulse with adrenaline. She confessed that her mind had taken over and she just knew that there was a gang of heroin addicts or something like that on the other side of that door, squatting in my apartment and using it as their own personal toilet while they rode their binge. No such luck.

She found the courage to open the door, cell phone in hand and ready to call police just in case her hunch had been correct. The light flipped on without any sort of reaction or response from me. Mom had paused in the doorway, trying to understand what it was she was looking at. To have her tell it, she could discern that it was me, but so much was wrong with the scene. I was wrapped in blankets and covers, bottles of both water and NyTime covered the mattress and wrappers of protein bars were littered throughout the rest of the bed area.

She dropped her phone as the site began to register in her head. The horrid smell coupled with the lack of any reaction from me once the light came on lead her to the conclusion that her son was dead. She screamed, still there was no reaction from me. She bent down to pick up her phone to call the cops, her legs gave out and she found herself on the floor, crying and searching blindly with her arms to find her phone. She was unable to take her eyes away from me as I lay there.

She found her phone and dialed 911 as she began to crawl toward my body. Whoever was on the other end of the line kept insisting that Mom calm down and try to explain what was happening and what was needed. She finally got the words out that she found her son unresponsive in his apartment and to send an ambulance. It was right around that moment that my eyes became squinted and my head lifted toward her. She let out another scream.

"When you think you are looking at a dead body the scariest thing you can see is movement," she later told the cops at the hospital. The hospital, by the way, is where I woke up. I found myself again in a bed connected to machines that monitored my heart and other functions. I woke up with a needle in my arm feeding me nutrients and re-hydrating me. In those 5 days of sleep, my only nutrition had been water and a half-dozen of those protein bars. I had dropped a considerable amount of weight by the time they had first admitted me and was severely dehydrated.

My eyes opened to a light brighter than I had ever seen. Light enveloped everything in that room and screamed at me as my eyes squinted and fought to adjust. After several minutes I could make out the shapes of my parents standing there in nearly the same positions as they had after the wreck. Exhausted concern was stretched across their faces as I turned my head to look at them.

"Oh Sam," my mother's tone filled with equal parts worry and disappointment.

"I know, M-" I started before my father interrupted.

"You have no clue, boy!" there were no mixed messages in his tone, he was angry. He didn't raise his voice, but that voice was saturated with intensity.

"You have no idea what you've put us through. Not just your mother and I, but everyone that cares about you! Now I don't know what you were thinking but I sure as hell know what you've done and how it's effected the people around you."

"Dad..."

"No Sam. Listen, I've paid off what was left on your lease, we are storing your stuff and you are moving back to the house."

"Sam," my mother started in, "I explained to the doctors here what happened, how I found you. They want you to speak to a professional about it, about Melody, the wreck, these scars they found on your body that none of us can explain, all of it."

"Mom, I don't-"

"Sam, we don't care what you want or think right now, you've lost it and you need help."

Silence hung in the air until a doctor walked in. We all watched as the middle-aged man sat down on the bed next to me. He looked around the room, acknowledged my parents before looking me in the eye.

"So you're Sam?" An unusual statement from a man that was supposed to know who he was treating.

I stared at him through my confusion and eventually responded:

"Yes."

"Ok...good to meet you. I have been trying to get you to wake up for a little while now, I am glad to see you decided to join us."

I nodded slightly, still perplexed by this man's demeanor.

"I am sure you thought you knew what you were doing or what you were trying to do. The thing is you put yourself at a huge risk and a lot of people who care about you are very concerned. It's not up to me to talk to you about the ins and outs of why you did what you did or what it was you were trying to do...but I do need to know if you are going to do it again."

"No sir."

"That was mostly meant as rhetoric...the point is that we are going to have a psychologist come and speak with you to determine if it is safe to let you leave here."

"Ok."

The doctor stood up, looked around, again acknowledging my folks, and left the room after they thanked him.

We stayed there in the room for an hour before the psychologist showed up. She was a young and beautiful woman. She sat next to me in a manner similar to the previous doctor. Her gaze met mine with more sympathy than any I had received so far that day.

"Sam."

"Yes."

"I am Dr. Reynolds, I want to talk to you about what has happened."

"I ummm...I don't know where to start."

"Ok, good."

"Good?"

"You're willing to talk."

"I wasn't trying to hurt myself."

"Were you trying to kill yourself?"

"Of course not."

"Please don't downplay everyone's concerns."

"I wasn't trying to."

"Of course not."

I stopped to think about what my next words to her would be. She must've seen the cogs in my mind spinning because she sat there and waited for me to respond.

"I didn't know how to deal with some things in my life. I felt more comfortable when I was asleep. I didn't hurt except for when I woke up and had to live. I had some time I could take from work...so I took it and I wanted to sleep as much as I could. That was the only place I could go to get away from the pain I feel."

There was silence while Dr. Reynolds took down some notes and studied me from her seated position.

"Sam. What you did put you in a very serious situation with your health. You didn't eat anything substantial or drink anything that could sustain you for a matter of days. Had you not been found when you had been, a lot of minds think that you could have caused yourself more severe and even permanent damage."

"I'm sorry."

"I am sure that you are."

"No...None of this was what I had intended."

"I also understand that you have some scarring on your body that was not there the last time you were examined."

"I stopped doing that a while ago."

"So they are self-inflicted?"

"Yes."

"Why?"

"To try to cope."

"With what?

"The same thing that I was trying to cope with by sleeping."

"Melody?"

"Yes."

"Your parents told me about her and what you have all been going through."

"I told you I stopped."

"I believe you. These scars are older than just a few weeks. Those aren't my concern as much as what it is that brought you to the hospital this time."

"Doctor, you really don't have to worry, I won't be doing this again."

"Good. But I have to worry, I can't just go on the word of the guy that landed himself here in the first place. So, here's what is going to happen. I will allow your release from the hospital whenever the other doctors recommend it. In return I need to you to speak with another psychologist, an old friend of mine, ok?"

"Who?"

"His name is Dr. Roberts, he was my mentor when I was first starting out. I will give his contact information to your parents and I recommend that you go see him within the next week.

"I will."

"Sam. He's going to help you but you have got to be honest with him. You know better than anyone else what it is that you are going through, his job will be to help you navigate what it is you feel and to find the best way to live with it and work through it."

"I know."

"Sam. This is serious. Please go see him."

I smiled a little and looked her again in the eye.

"Ok...for you then."

It was three days between leaving the hospital seeing Dr. Roberts. That first full day at home, back at my parents' place was hell. I checked out of the hospital after paying another visit to Melody. I sat there in the room with her and told her I loved her and everything else that had happened, that I was going to see a shrink. I sat there with her for as long as my folks could stand to wait and then we left. That drive back was as silent as the first time months ago after the wreck. There were boxes of the few hastily packaged things grabbed from my apartment sitting haphazardly throughout the living room. My dad told me that my furniture was being moved to a storage unit and whatever clothes or other items I may need we could go get together the next day.

We ate dinner in a cautioned silence, my parents trying to anticipate anything I may say and trying desperately to let me say those things without being coerced. That first night I slept on the couch having decided to avoid my room with the window that peered right into Melody's, to avoid my room full of memories. I know I had been in the room since the wreck and had learned how to exist inside of it, but that first night I knew my nerves would still be too raw and my pain too exposed. I would wait until Max came over the next evening to face the room and in that room I would allow myself to stay after he left, but not a moment sooner.

The morning of that second day my father and I went to my apartment, the stench was still there. I grabbed my clothes from the closet and various drawers and loaded them into my dad's car. While we were there some men from a moving company came and asked what to pack up and load.

"All of it I suppose," was the only answer I could think to give.

My dad and I stayed around for about an hour to supervise the moving crew. I packed pictures and took things off of the walls and tried to keep things as organized as I could. By the time we left my home had been mostly emptied, a hollow and stinky mess...just like me.

We followed the moving truck to the storage building and watched as they stacked all of my stuff, my whole life outside of her, into what was essentially a giant closet. The mood was somber and despite the sunny day...there seemed to be a cloud made from a million droplets of sadness hanging over us. The day would continue on like this until Max came over later that night. When people worry they all seem to wear the same damn look on their faces, one of pity and concern and of fear...none of these things I wanted for myself...all of these things needed to be aimed at Melody...the true victim. I was stealing the attention she deserved and that was the furthest thing from what I had wanted.

The doorbell rang, it would be Max. I opened the door and before there had been enough time for his face to sink into that same damn pitiful expression as everyone else, I slapped him. Not hard...just enough to prevent his face from finishing that look. He looked at me through a furrowed brow for a moment, trying to figure out what had just happened. I stood there motionless and void of expression, watching him as he stewed over my actions before slapping me in return. I turned my body toward the inside of the house to invite Max in, he crept by me without taking his eyes off of mine, unblinking and cautious. Once he was in the house far enough I closed the door behind him and gave him a hug. He put his arms around me and we stood there embracing, letting go of the stinging in our faces.

Max lifted his eyes toward the upstairs and slightly lifted his head, letting me know he wanted to chat in my room. We went up the stairs and we found our usual places in the room. He looked at me and asked simply: "Why?"

"Max," I started in, "I don't know."

"Bullshit. I know you and I know you wouldn't try to kill yourself."

"Is that what they told you?"

"That's what it looked like."

"It's not...that's not what happened."

"Then tell me what the hell you were thinking!"

Silence.

"I'm going to see a shrink...to talk to somebody about it."

"Ok...will you tell him what this is all about?"

"You know what this is about, Max."

"Melody?! You gotta be kidding me with that, Sam...do you think this is what she would want you to do? Huh? You think she wants you hurting yourself?! Scarring yourself? This whole mess with how your mom found you...you think she would want ANY of that?"

I had no answer that he would want to hear.

"Max I'm sorry."

"I know...we all know...I'm just worry about you...we are all scared."

"We should be more worried about Melody."

"Melody isn't self-destructing."

"Neither am I....I just…I'm trying to be ok."

More silence.

"I'm gonna go talk to this shrink in a couple of days...I'm sure that'll help."

"Yeah...is there anything I can do? Anything you need from me, Sam?"

"No. We need to focus on Melody."

"Mel is fine, she is exactly where she needs to be right now."

I looked at Max; that statement didn't sound like anything he would normally say.

"That's what my dad says."

The fact that I still knew him so well made me smile, it was a genuine smile and one that spread to Max's face as well.

We spent a little while longer in my room, talking about Melody and discussing Max's plans for the upcoming semester and so on before returning downstairs. We found my parents in the living room watching some home-makeover show. It still struck me as odd when I would come across the people in my life going about their lives as normal. I am sure that Melody was never too far from their minds, and it was a testament to their own mental stability that they could recognize their own need to continue in normalcy, a trait that I needed to try and find within myself.

Two days had passed since I had slapped Max. In those two days we spent as much time together as we could. I knew he needed me and he knew I needed to not be stuck in that hospital as much as I had been. In those two days we had begun to forge a bond deeper than ever, one that could only be established by shared grief. Somehow we built upon that life-long relationship, somehow we became more than brothers.

I confided in him, nearly everything. I had told him that I had scarred myself in the hopes of being able to better understand the changes Melody had undergone. I told him that everything I had done had been to try and better understand her and her current state. I told him it was his father that had once told me the only way to make a marriage work is to 'change together' and that the things I had done were my best bet at doing so.

Although I told him all of these things I never told him about my connection with Melody. I never brought myself to share with him that she would visit me in my dreams as long as I had stayed medicated. I knew exactly how that sounded and I believed that if I had told him, or anyone for that matter, I would have ended up in a lot more trouble than just having to see a psychologist.

Max didn't agree with any of it, but he listened. He told me that those extremes were unhealthy and not at all what his father had intended. We never argued about it, I knew how he felt and I had proof of my own conviction. Instead Max supported me in my 'decision' to go see the shrink; Dr. Roberts. Max knew I was hesitant about opening up to someone about the things that had happened, the things I had done, the things I was still trying to go through, and he reassured me at any sign of concern that this was the right thing to do both for me and for Melody.

I left the house early on my way to Dr. Robert's office. I wanted to have some time to drive around and maybe put together some thoughts on what to say. I had assumed that he would have been brought up to speed on everything and that what he, my folks, the hospital people, the Black's wanted to hear was an explanation regarding my actions.

I drove around for a bit, unable to decide on anything. I had turned off the radio to better hear myself think, I had thought about this meeting from so many different angles: If I approach my time with Dr. Roberts as I have with everyone else then I could get away with having just made some poor decisions in their eyes. If I were completely honest with the shrink and told him that I felt like I could communicate with Melody while under the spell of medicine, who knows what would happen next?

I eventually found myself in the parking lot having decided to be open with Dr. Roberts. Regardless of who Dr. Roberts actually was, this person represented the opportunity to come clean and mend my conscience and that was an opportunity I could not pass up this time.

I sat in the lobby, anxiously waiting for someone to call my name and usher me to whatever room I was supposed to go to. My body remained remarkably still considering my high level of anxiety. I felt no need to flip through magazines or tap my feet or look around. I sat there. I waited.

They called my name and I stood up and followed them to a room that over the next few months would become very familiar. The room itself was small in dimension but had been decorated to resemble the living room of a upper-middle-class household, designed to welcome and evoke comfort without being too clean or inaccessible.

Dr. Roberts came in only a few short minutes after I had sat down in the room. He was an average looking middle-aged man neither too tall nor short nor round nor slender. He was aware of his hairline and made up for that by growing out a short but well-kept beard. Beyond those initial and obvious physical attributes I could not gain a bead on what this man might have been into in his personal life. By looking at him he very well could have been athletic in his younger incarnation. He was conventionally attractive and occupationally successful so I could assume he had a wife and (with no supporting evidence) I liked to think he had a daughter who may have been late in her high-school career...17...maybe 18 years old.

For being someone I was about to spill very intimate and damning information to, I had incredibly little knowledge of who he was outside of speculation and I doubted in those introductory moments that Dr. Roberts would have much interest in sharing any of who he is with me.

"Samuel Merritt." His first words to me.

"Sam." My first to him.

"I am Dr. Roberts, it's nice to meet you."

I nodded and smiled to return the sentiment.

"So why don't you tell me why you are here."

"You already know."

"Why do you say that?"

"You asked me to tell you about my situation...what brought me here instead of telling you about myself. That tells me you know already about my situation but want to hear my view of it for purposes of comparison...right?"

"So why don't you tell me about yourself, Sam."

Momentary silence.

"Sorry Doc, I didn't mean to sound like such a jerk. I have every intention of cooperating and telling you whatever you want to know."

"Sam the reason you are here is not to tell me what I want to know. You are here so that we can figure out some things together."

"What things?"

He lit up and replied, "That's a great place to start."

With that tone he might as well have said 'Checkmate.' He had a calm and nearly proud sense about him and after those first few exchanges I felt very at ease with him.

"Can we start by you telling me what you already know?"

The idea of beginning our first session with him laying his cards on the table made him uncertain. He studied me for a moment as I studied him. I was sure that I had not yet won his confidence or comfort in the same way he had so quickly won mine.

He began:

"I know the clinical details of what has happened. I know that you have been cutting and burning parts of your body and that you had been admitted to a hospital due to severe dehydration that resulted from what can be considered a staggering binge on over-the-counter sleep medication."

"Do you know why?"

"I think you should tell me about the 'why', Sam."

"I lost someone."

"Who did you lose?"

That question lingered in my mind for a few minutes. Dr. Roberts did not push me to answer quickly, he was not a man that was made uncomfortable by silence; he appreciated a well-thought answer over a knee-jerk reaction.

"There's so much to say, so much to cover and explain."

"We will get to it. For next time I want you to think about where a good place to start will be."

"Next time?"

"Yes, I'm going to recommend that we end for the day now that you and I have formally met and you can take a few days to put together your thoughts."

"That's it?"

"For today."

Silence lingered again for a few moments before he continued.

"Come back early next week if that works for you and tell me about where you believe this all started."

I nodded again with a smile.

"Very good," he stood and I followed, "Sam it was nice to get to meet you and I will look forward to seeing you again."

With that he led me to the lobby area and told me to schedule the next appointment with June at the front desk. I did just that and drove home in silence, replaying as best I could the events of my first meet with Dr. Roberts.

The weekend came and I spent my time either with my parents or with Max, my thoughts never far removed from what I was going to talk to Dr. Roberts about come Tuesday.

Tuesday came and I began my trek to see Dr. Roberts. I had done as he had asked and spent a considerable amount of time putting together some thoughts on where this whole chapter in my life began. For as ready and willing as I was to divulge and confide, I was not looking forward to this one bit.

I had a chat with my dad between last week's meeting and today. He was curious about what was said, how I felt, all the usual stuff you would expect from a caring father. He was happy to hear that I was willing and even wanting to participate in the 'therapy' despite my own trepidations. One thing I did take away from our talk (the one I had with my dad) was that often pain is the path we have to travel in order to reach a better state. This would certainly be a path of pain.

I parked my car in the same spot as last time and followed the same path to the door, to the lobby, to the chair in the lobby. I sat there motionless and filled with a similar anxiety as I had before. My wait lasted only a few minutes before being taken to the same small room as before, silly as it may sound I found that comforting.

I sat down in the same chair as last time and Dr. Roberts joined me a few minutes after. I watched as he gently closed the door and found his way to his seat. He crossed his legs almost immediately and then he asked how I was. We spent a few minutes on pleasantries before picking up where we had left off.

I told him I believed all of this had started with the wreck. I described what I could of the moments surrounding the event and what came after.

"...Yeah Doc, the beeps."

He was taking notes, I would stop from time to time to give a moment to catch up to my lengthy responses and ramblings; something he often asked me not to do. He assured me several times that listening while writing was something he is a 'pro' at.

He looked up at me in the middle of this silence, one that lasted longer than my usual 'let him catch up' silences. He could tell my wheels were turning and I was looking for how to say my next words.

"What's on your mind, Sam?'"

I sat there for another moment, trying to put my thoughts together in a coherent sentence.

"I spent so much time thinking about what to say to you, how to describe everything, how to put it all into words. Now I can't seem to think of the things I wanted to say." I broke that thought with a small laugh before continuing on. "I wish I had written it down."

"So do that."

"Do what?"

"I'm going to give you something to think about and to mull-over in between our time together, just like I did last week in asking you to tell me where you think all of this began, and I want you to write down your thoughts."

"And what...like turn it in to you like homework?"

"No...Not at all...it will be a journal of sorts for your eyes only. If you want to bring it with you and use it as a tool to remember things then great...but if nothing else it should help you focus on what it is you want to say."

"I dunno, Doc."

"It's not an order, just a recommendation Sam...But I do think it would help."

"I'll think about it."

"So you woke up in the hospital? Those were the beeps?"

We spent the rest of our hour together talking about the hospital and my reactions to seeing Melody for the first time after the collision. The hour ended with Dr. Roberts telling me he wanted me to think back to the wreck itself. He said if that was the beginning of all of this then he wanted me to try and remember as much detail about it as I could. He made his suggestion again about buying a note pad and jotting down some thoughts. We shook hands again and I followed him as he led me to the lobby to schedule my next appointment.

As it turns out on certain days of the week after a certain hour, a different woman comes and takes care of the receptionist duties. I hadn't noticed her until I got looked up toward the desk on my approach...and then for just a few moments...I couldn't stop noticing her; her name was Grace She asked me when I wanted to set my next appointment and we decided on the same time next week.

I drove home and spent the evening with my parents. Mom made dinner and as a family we sat around the table eating and discussing how things went today with Dr. Roberts. I have to admit that even having only met with the man twice, I felt that I was better able to communicate certain things to my parents. I still had no intention of telling them the things I had planned to tell Dr. Roberts, but knowing that I at least planned to be honest with someone made it all the more easy to speak to other people in whatever capacity I deemed fitting or necessary.

They had known from our conversations leading up to my appointment that Dr. Roberts wanted me to try and surmise the origin of this shit storm and relate that to him in my own words. They knew I had dedicated some time to piecing all that together, and I told them that I had difficulty putting into words with him things I had previously cobbled together mentally. They enjoyed Dr. Robert's idea of a 'journal' to record thoughts to help my recall and they cautioned me about spending too much time trying to remember the events of the wreck itself. They acknowledged that the exercise was at the request of a professional but were quick to remind me that they knew better than just about anyone...we all knew what they meant by 'just about.'

The night concluded with some TV and discussions about our next trip to see Melody. I went to my room around 10 and lay in bed with a calm and steady mind trying to think about the night of the wreck. I focused on the details I could remember, the ones I had given to the cops a few months ago the morning after it happened. I fought to keep my mind trained on the wreck, to try and decipher flashes of images that would return to me but everything led me back to her, back to Melody.

I became angry at the fact that I couldn't do more, angry that she was comatose and I was sentenced only to seeing a shrink. I was angry that all of my attempts to make things right and to atone for this horrible event for which no one held me responsible and brought me no further than the illusion of a connection to her through mutilation and codeine abuse. My mind splintered into a thousand different directions, each thought as fleeting and painful and angry as the next. Hours had passed and I struggled to turn my mind off. I lay there in silence trying now to think of nothing, trying to give in to the stillness of the air that surrounded me, trying not to wonder if my mother had thought to take away the bottle of NyTime that was usually kept behind my mirror. She had. Sleep would eventually find me...and she was restless.

I woke up late the following morning from a night of tossing and turning, my mind unable to lock on to any single thing long enough to have dreamed, my sheets a mess and nearly as tangled as my hair.

I climbed out of bed and ventured down the hallway and began my descent of the stairs. From the second-to-bottom-stair I could see on the kitchen's island a few items that had been set out for me. My mother, however many hours ago had poured me a dry bowl of cereal and a glass of orange juice that certainly by now would now be room temperature. As I approached the island my still-blurry eyes were able to focus enough to figure out that she had also set out for me a notebook and pen. The cover of the notebook read in my mother's handwriting 'The Journey of Sam Merritt."

I smiled and thought to myself how intuitive and loving of a woman she really is. The gesture symbolized not only their support in my 'treatment' with Dr. Roberts, but their hopefulness and belief in who I was. I poured milk over my cereal and sat there staring at the book, crunching and thinking. I finished breakfast and grabbed the pen and pages and returned to my room. I thought so hard about writing. I thought about thinking. I was still stressed from my thoughts from the night before that I couldn't bring myself to conjure those things again. I decided to retreat from the moment and call Max. He was about to leave to go see Melody and invited me to join him.

I spent that trip focused on Max. I had continued to go visit Melody every day just as I always had. I still believed she knew when I was there and when I was not, and it was that belief that allowed me to watch over Max on this particular day. I knew she was there with us, I could feel her just as though she was standing next to me, our mutual love and concern for her brother overtaking us both. I watched as he approached her side and whispered something to her. Max began to cry and though my curiosity was piqued, my sense of brotherhood drew me to him as we shared a hug.

I waited for Max to tell me what was on his mind or heart or conscience, whichever had been the source of his tears but he said nothing and so I asked nothing. He didn't heave, he didn't bellow, he simply wept for a few moments. After those moments had passed and he pulled his head away from my shoulder, my eyes met his and they conveyed gratitude and contentment. We stayed only a little while longer;

a total time of maybe 20 minutes. As we got to his Jeep I suggested grabbing some lunch and we made our way to a burger place that was nearby. Max eventually broke the silence by telling me what had brought on his emotions from earlier.

Max seemed to be on the opposite end of the spectrum from me when it came to her state-of-awareness. He confided in me that when he is there in the room with her she feels far away, further than she ever had. He told me that after the accident for weeks and weeks he would dream about her consistently; that he still felt connected to her as he always had and that now he rarely dreams, and no longer about her. To use his words he felt he was losing his 'Super-twin-powers' that they used to share.

My hypocrisy had never been more apparent to me than it was after I began to attempt consoling him. I began by telling him that a bunch of stuff that he already knew; that I have never had a twin so I can't know what that type of bond and connection must feel like. I told him strictly in that sense I was the outsider of our group and that even though I had no ground to stand on, in my opinion, people don't have those types of connections...that there are no 'Super-twin-powers.'

To my shame I found it easier to shoot down and discredit a large part of the foundation upon which my best friend and his sister (the woman I believed could talk to me if I were medicated and asleep)'s relationship than to tell him that truth. I spent the next few moments trying to mend some of the wounds I had inflicted upon him without trying to take back any of what I had said. I told him that I believed Melody was still in there and that she would come back to us. I told him to not give up hope but to be realistic about his own expectations. I was full of shit and in being given the opportunity to help my friend, I had instead pushed him further down for believing in something he could not logically explain. I had lost such an integral part of what made me who I believed myself to be; I had lost my empathy, I had lost my ability to truly care for the people closest to me and I had become someone I would be ashamed to show Melody.

The guilt over that conversation and the false revelations I tried to give to Max were the final push that I needed to begin what would become my next and final trial of atonement.

While Max was confident enough in himself and his love for his sister, he was still impressionable enough to not mention his feelings about their connection for quite some time.

We spent a few more hours together at his house, playing old video games from our childhood and at a few points even laughing together about one thing or another. I wanted so badly to apologize to him but my pride and my fear would not allow it. We made plans to hang out in a couple of days and I made my way home, inwardly sulking and weighed down by the pain I had caused him.

My parents were in the kitchen sipping on wine as I passed by them and headed again up the stairs to my room. They stopped me to say hello and make sure I had found the notebook that had been left for me. I let them know that I had and that I was going to go and work on putting some thoughts on paper for next week's session with Dr. Roberts. Their smiles turned to stone-faced expressions in the attempt to show concern and seriousness toward the task. I thanked them for the book and continued on my way.

The door closed behind me and I sat on my bed cross-legged with a blank page staring up at me. I thought heavily about what it was I needed to remember. Things flashed in my mind like a light bulb flickering on and blinking away as it dies. I had images, some that were as clear as day and others that I could feel desperately trying to break to the foreground of my mind.

I began to jot down simple one or two or three word phrases and thoughts as I played and replayed and replayed the scene in my head. By the time I had filled a few pages with scratches and scribbling of small moments I finally began to write. I wrote what I could as a narrative and that seemed to work for me better than bits and pieces incoherently spewed between lines on a page.

I began writing about driving with Melody after the dinner we had shared with our families to celebrate our engagement.

SEE APPENDIX 1

Time that would have been spent that week trying to figure out what I wanted to tell the shrink was now devoted to reading and re-reading those words. I had never really tried to write anything meaningful and the words that ended up on the page after those few hours that night were the first of many that were to come.

The conversations I had with Melody over those next few days, the thoughts I would send to her while I sat at her side, were largely centered around my feelings about writing in the notebook. I held her hand and let her know that I was able to remember more of the wreck than before and that as incredibly painful as the experience of reliving those moments had been, there was some catharsis in it.

I had found that even after just that one night of writing my time with Melody felt more complete. I felt that I had accomplished something meaningful and for the first time, healthy. I felt close to her again. It had been a couple of weeks since my mother had found me strung out in bed on NyTime and thus it had been a couple of weeks since I felt my connection to Mel. While writing was not a replacement for that same experience, it was something productive and something that so far had seemed to help.

My time with Max was less heavy on the heart and my time with my parents seemed to be more open and less bound by the constraints of shame over my previous actions. There still was a terrible burden that I felt, but I think exploring that, which is what I had done through that journal, helped me to immerse myself in and focus on that burden for periods instead of carrying it around at all times. Melody was never far away from whatever was on my mind, but at least for now the guilt felt manageable.

The following Tuesday came and I returned yet again to meet with Dr. Roberts. Journal in hand I went through the process of checking in and waiting in the lobby, being called back to the small room and waiting for him to come in. In typical fashion he arrived and sat down. I wondered if he could sense the excitement beaming out of my eyes at what I had accomplished. I wanted to wait and see what his first words would be, I didn't want to tip my hand just yet.

"How was your week, Sam?"

"It was good."

"I see you brought a notebook with you."

"Yes and I love it...it's been a tremendous help." I may have shown him my cards.

Dr. Roberts smiled at my exuberance.

"Good. I'm glad to hear that you gave it a shot."

"I did. In fact it helped me remember some things I couldn't previously...remember."

"Tell me about that."

I explained to him the process in which I wrote that night, starting with words or phrases and eventually writing it out as a sort of story. I waited for him to ask if he could see it, to ask if he could read the words I had written but he never did. Instead I handed him the book and asked him to look it over. He paused for a moment and asked if I was sure he wanted me to read these things, which I was, and he flipped through it.

"How did you feel while you were writing this, Sam?"

I actually had to stop and think about that answer.

"I dunno, Doc. I don't remember feeling any certain way...once it started, I kept on until it was done, and...that was it."

"You weren't emotional? Anger...sadness...anything like that?"

"No...I was just...in it...that's the best way I can think to explain it. Was I supposed to be emotional?"

"Sam the only aim of having you write things down was to help you remember for our sessions together the things you wanted to say...if you found some other meaning and help behind it...that's just fine."

Dr. Robert's underwhelming response "that's just fine" felt like having the rug pulled out from under me. I had been so hyped up about the way writing in the book had made me feel, and I guess without realizing it I had hoped to validate that fervor with the approval of the man who was trying to help me through this. While he didn't disapprove of what I had created, I now felt alone in my excitement.

"Why do you think writing helped?"

"I don't know Doc...when I was writing, I felt completely surrounded by the moments. I felt I was re-living those moments. I felt connected to them."

"Was it a connection you were looking for when you were cutting yourself? When you were self-medicating?"

"That was different. When I was scarring myself it was never just to cause pain. The point in that whole thing was to try and undergo the same changes Melody went through."

"Sam, there is no way for you to know what she has gone through, what she is going through. No more than she can understand what you are going through."

"So then what's the difference if it makes me feel less guilty?"

"The difference, Sam is that you are still able to communicate, you still have family and friends and now me to communicate to when you are struggling. The difference is that you aren't bound by the same things that bind her."

"How am I supposed to communicate my feelings to my family and friends and to you when no one blames me for what has happened?"

"You blame yourself?

"Yes...and no one else will."

"Have you stopped to think that the reason for that is because what happened wasn't your fault, maybe there was no way to save her from what happened?"

"That may be the case but for whatever reason it doesn't change the fact that I feel guilty...if not for the wreck..." my voice trailed off as I sought the rest of that sentence.

"For surviving."

"Yes! I've tried to figure out how to say it...that's exactly it...for not being in the car with her."

"That is called Survivor's Guilt."

"Ok."

"It's not uncommon for someone who comes away from a tragedy to go through a certain period of re-evaluation...of self, of others, of values, etc. When there is loss involved, if someone passes away-"

"She's not dead."

"Which can make things even more difficult. When there is no body to bury, no ending point, no period at the end of the sentence it can be more difficult to move beyond the experience and instead one might cherish the guilt in lieu of the person until such a time as a conclusion is discovered."

"Very clinical."

"It helps to know what you are facing Sam."

"But it changes nothing. She is still where I can't get to her, and the only times I have felt connected to her at all have been when I've destroyed myself."

"Do you truly believe that she will wake up, son?"

"Yes I do."

"Then you need to realize that if you continue to 'destroy yourself,' there won't be anything left of you when she comes back."

A few minutes passed by as I processed what had been said. Dr. Roberts continued to write his notes.

"I recommend you find some productive outlet to invest your energy in instead of guilt."

"Model airplanes? Doc no matter what I do she is going to be on my mind."

"So utilize that for something. You said writing helps, try to keep writing the things you feel...maybe that will help you confront the burden you are carrying."

"What do you want me to write about?"

He thought for a few moments, knowing that last week I had written about the darkness and trauma of the wreck.

"Try to think of your best memory with Melody. Think about a moment that stands out to you as being a defining moment in your relationship. Think of something happy and put it into words."

See appendix 2

That entry came a few nights after my appointment with Dr. Roberts. That was the moment I was supposed to write about, the greatest connection I had ever felt to Melody, put into words as best as I knew how. The night I wrote that I slept so well, I felt at peace with a lot of things.

That night I dreamed of her the way I used to when I would self-medicate. She already knew about Dr. Roberts and the journal from the things I have told her during my visits to the hospital. It had been weeks since I had seen her in my dreams and when I woke up the next day I felt wonderful.

My appointments had now become something of a regularly scheduled event, every Tuesday. Between the last Tuesday and the one that was coming up I went back to that journal and wrote several more times. Each time I was able to tap into some different memory or experience that had happened with Melody or Max or the three of us and every time I went back to writing I was able to better articulate each memory I had.

Those journal entries were later used to write the first parts of this story. It was because of those journal entries that I began to finally learn to accept what was happening. I wrote about more recent events like my scarring and burning and self-medicating, nothing was out of my reach so long as I was extracting things from my mind and putting pen to paper.

Dr. Roberts had been pleased with our time together over the next three weeks; before leaving his office he told me that he could see a marked difference in my demeanor, in my ability to communicate what I was going through and dealing with. He never asked to see my journal and I never offered it to him, but because of that journal I had found a new voice.

It was that voice, however, that soon became its own character; its own damning force that would take over in a very similar way the scarring and the burning and the self-medicating had. As with the other tools I had utilized to cope with Melody's situation, this soon became a destructive force in my attempt to accept what was in front of me.

I became consumed with the idea again that Melody was fully aware of what was happening and could connect with me through my dreams; so long as I continued to write. Dr. Roberts attributed what happened over the next several weeks to my guilt, as per usual. I'm sure he was right but during that time I did not care. He made the case that only when I made some attempt to compensate for Melody's condition was I able to feel truly connected to her. He said that when I attacked my guilt through physically detrimental means my psyche fabricated a connection to her to help justify the continuation of that guilt. He told me I was building myself into 'an imperfect fortress', a structure founded on what he called 'unreason' and built solely for the purpose of its inevitable collapse.

In a single one-week span I was able to fill up half of a notebook. It was a couple of completely-filled notebooks and 3 weeks later that I let go and gave into my guilt to begin my final trial. I had given a lot of thought to the things my parents and Dr. Roberts had said, about there being no way for me to truly understand what Melody had gone through, what her experiences were. I had listened when they told me that there was no reality in the notion that it was truly Melody in my dreams communicating with me, that it was all part of my stressed out mind and body. I knew there was no way to convince them of what I felt and what I believed, I knew that they would never support what I was about to do but nonetheless my convictions drove me to continue.

In those first weeks Melody was always in my dreams so long as I had been writing, but she was, every time, muted. I spent hours by her side in the hospital, speaking silently to her and asking why she wouldn't talk to me, why I couldn't hear her. I realized eventually as I sat at her bedside that she wanted to communicate with me, but that I was not able to hear her over my own voice. I knew then that my final act of atonement would be silence.

For the next few days I focused on what it meant to be silent. Melody was unable to communicate in any way and I knew that I could not replicate that to an extent that would be desired. It was the same issue as with the mutilating and medicating; I was unable to put myself into a coma, so what could I do to help understand what it would be like to not communicate?

I decided that until Melody either wakes up or dies, I would be silent. I would not speak until such a time as a conclusion to her condition would be known. As Dr. Roberts had stated about Survivor's Guilt, ' When there is no body to bury, no ending point, no period at the end of the sentence it can be more difficult to move beyond the experience and instead one might cherish the guilt in lieu of the person until such a time as a conclusion is discovered.'

I know what I did made no sense to anyone except for me, but how many people can say they haven't made some choice in their life that was beyond the mental grasp of their support system?

I was met with resistance from all sides; my folks, Dr. Roberts, the Black family, but my resolve was as steadfast as it had been with my previous trials. I spent time sorting out what was allowable and what was not. I would not speak a word until we knew Mel's fate. I would keep my journal as it helped me in my communications with her, I would keep my phone so people could text me, though I would not respond unless it was a true emergency or if there was some development with Melody.

That first week was hell. If you have never tried to go any measurable length of time without speaking...I don't recommend it. The act itself of staying quiet goes so far beyond not responding to others. Speaking can be such a knee-jerk reaction to any number of things; you bless someone after they sneeze, you say hi to strangers as you pass them by, the hardest one for me was catching the 'Huh?' that comes out of my mouth like a caveman when someone I'm not paying attention to asks me a question.

Max figured that out almost right away and was relentless in his attempts to get me to break my silence. At first I was so upset with him for trying to get me to slip up or to abort the trial completely, but eventually I embraced it as his concern for me and it became something of a game between us. He didn't understand what it was I was trying to accomplish but I sense that in time he had grown to understand the 'why.'

My parents were angry and concerned. My mother was scared of finding me drugged up and passed out on my bed again, scared that her sweet son was hurting himself and didn't know how to ask for help. My father told me he was disappointed that his boy would react so immaturely and selfishly in such an important time. When it came down to it, I found I was able to embrace their anger much more easily than their disappointment.

Melody's parents never expressed anything but concern. I think they saw me as a puppy sitting at the door after his owners have left to go to work or the grocery store or something. The only times they really saw me were at the hospital as I sat next to their daughter. To them I sat there still and silent and mourning when in truth I was talking to their daughter in a way that only I could. I was the only one that could get through to her; now more completely than ever.

My time with Dr. Roberts had become very interesting. I began my code of silence on a Tuesday at midnight. I chose that time so that I could have one final session with him. I was not surprised that he advised strongly against what I had set out to do, what shocked me was that he still wanted to see me the following week. At the time I thought he wanted me to return that next week because he did not believe I could last 7 days without speaking. I would later find out that his reasoning for the continuation of our time together was not for that reason, but instead to monitor and assess my obviously questionable mental stability and its effect on my physical well-being.

Tuesday came; those 7 days had passed and I had written notes throughout the week to provide him with some insight into how things were. I told him about Max and how he perpetually tried to get me to break, about my parents' anger and disappointment and about the concerned stares I would get from the rest of the Black family.

In these next several pages I have included the journal entries from this period, my trial of silence. The pages and entries I have put in here will reflect and hopefully illustrate my mental state as the days progressed and my mind unraveled.

see appendix 3

Everything changed today. I went to the mall...it was common, unremarkable, routine.

Except...

I had walked the top and bottom floors a few lazy times. I peered through windows of shops and listened to people when I wanted.

I climbed the stairs to the top level for another pass and then time slowed down. For the next several minutes I was without the thought of the past several months. I saw her from across a distance. The receptionist from Dr. Robert's office; Grace. She had some guy draped around her...he looked like an undeserving piece of shit. I looked at her intensely and with purpose. She looked happy when she saw me. She always seemed like the type to be troubled but put on a brave face. I could see that in her...that she was never far removed from a bad memory...maybe someone touching her in a way she did not like...probably that guy she was with...I am sure that guy she was with contributed...he looked like trouble...like he was perpetually recovering...but she was smiling through it…not hiding it or hiding behind it or in it or beside it or in any other relation to it but…through it.

 She was close...we were close, still passing, slowly, I watched her mouth open and I could see her chest heave as she breathed in enough air to release a small and beautiful "hey."

Without a moment passing I slowly let out a very air-filled 'hhhi.' This pathetic, whimpering word had been the first that I…or anyone for that matter had heard from my throat in several weeks' time…and as soon as her radiance left me, I was frozen, I was left empty again, no…beyond empty. Not only was I forcefully thrust back into my loneliness, I was without the sanctity of my solemn promise.

It was at that next moment that my pocket began to vibrate, it was my phone, and somehow I knew what this phone call would be. Melody was awake. Melody was awake, and I had broken my promise that no one asked me to make, I had broken my promise to her, a promise that she was unaware of. How long had she been awake? Did I break before she woke up? After? Was she OK? What brought her back? Was it because I broke my promise?

My phone beeped, I now had 1 missed call and 1 voice mail.

It wasn't disbelief that had taken hold of me in the moments immediately following that message; no one in my family would be that cold-hearted. Maybe it was the order in which things had happened that led me to be so skeptical but I stood there enveloped in a moment of complete suspense. Nothing felt real as I stood there in the middle of that walkway, my mind screaming at me to get to her as quickly as possible and I couldn't get my legs to move.

It was her, my reaction to her, that broke my silence and in my state of shock she turned around and came back to start a conversation with me. She stood next to me waiting for me to acknowledge her as I had before but this time I was motionless. It was a few seconds after she asked me how I was that my head finally turned to her, unblinking. No words came out. I had, in fact, just re-discovered my ability to close my mouth. She looked at me, expecting some sort of response but all she received was me turning to walk away, to run away, back to the parking lot, to my car, to the hospital, to Melody.

I do not remember the drive; all I remember is entering her room and seeing her eyes light up as I am sure mine must have. I rushed to the side of her bed and hovered over her, my hands pouring over her face as tears streamed down mine. As I kissed her I could feel her lips trembling, trying to kiss me and I realized how weak she was. I pulled away from her as her father began to speak.

"Sam so many of her muscles have atrophied."

I turned back to her as she blinked at me as if to agree with what he had said.

"She has a long road of rehabilitation in front of her."

I struggled to speak, it felt as though I had lost some muscle as well.

"Wh...Is...is she going to be ok?"

Nothing could come out louder than a soft whisper.

I felt the hospital bed move slightly and I turn to look at her, she blinked at me again as if to answer my question.

"She isn't able to speak yet," her father continued, "between the coma and any possible trauma from removing the ventilator, she will have to build her voice back as well."

I could not tear my eyes away from her. She was back. She had returned to me. She was beautiful. I leaned in to kiss her forehead and she moved toward me; a miraculous feeling after these long and painful months of waiting.

The next several months passed much more quickly than the previous ones. Things had reconciled themselves in marvelous ways and Melody and I were back on track toward our wedding.

She fought so hard during her rehab to recapture the magic of things the rest of our families took for granted, and in turn watching her accomplish such relatively simple tasks like walking or holding small objects without shaking inspired all of us to be thankful. There were some lasting effects from the trauma of the wreck, and while those effects may never fade, I am even more in love with her because they symbolize all she had fought through to come back.

I had returned to meet with Dr. Roberts for several weeks after Melody's return. My ghastly physical appearance and unstable mental framework were gradually replaced by foundations more durable than before the accident. Much of our time together after Melody's return was spent examining the events that happened in my dreams and how they correlated to my mental and physical deterioration. Dr. Roberts had concluded that the beast I believed to symbolize Melody's coma was more than likely a mental construct that I had built to represent the challenge of my silence. His logic for this was fairly simple: as my life and physical health had become more troublesome, the monster grew in a corresponding manner both in size and in strength. The fact that those types of dreams went away after Melody awoke from her coma helped to support his theory as well.

By the time we stopped meeting on a weekly basis I had become a better man for her. The cocoon of my guilt had shed and I had emerged a different creature than I had previously been.

Melody had even joined me for a few sessions with the Doc. We discussed as a group the things that she went through during rehab and the merits of what it was I had tried to accomplish during my own trials. I was thankful that no one had told her about my scarring or self-medicating or my silence before our meeting with Dr. Roberts. She never tried to make me feel worse for what I had done though she was unable to tell me that it helped her in any sort of way while she was gone.

I struggled for a long time with the idea that I had been the reason Melody had come out of her coma. The thought that she seemingly woke up at the same moment I broke my silence weighed on me for some time. It was that type of coincidence that kept me believing in the connection I shared with her while she was comatose.

Melody could not recall anything during her time in the hospital before waking up and not once would she be able to cite her feelings about the wreck, having remembered not a single moment of it. Enough time has passed that I can rightfully admit to the errors of what I had done; at least to their motives. I hid behind her pain as an excuse to torture myself, no words will ever be able to express my shame for that. I can, however, own my actions and say with confidence that what I had done I had done to help myself cope, just as Dr. Roberts had stated many months ago.

As the wedding draws closer and Melody and I have picked up our life together from where we had left off, I remain struck by a moment that transpired a few weeks after we had moved into our new apartment.

Melody and I had just finished dinner and we had loaded the dishes into the dishwasher. She was cleaning a few things in the kitchen as I went to the couch and turned on the news. She finished what she was doing and sat next to me, nuzzled closely under my arm. I put my arm around her and gently kissed her forehead and asked her if she knew how much I loved her. Her response was perfect:

"To Infinity one thousand times over."

Absolute Zeroes

....

...ONe OF tHeSe dayS I WiLL Start payiNg atteNtioN to tHat daMN aLarM, tiMe to get uP

He sits up in cold sweat

HuH?! WHat'S tHere?

"what's"?...who asks that?

WH...WHo'S tHere?
...HMMMpH...Friday.
I Need Food, SHaKiNg, tHirSty, Starved..........
ApartMeNt iS eMpty, (eveN Food HaS goNe aWay) MuSt've beeN tHe LeFtovers OF tHat trip. I reMeMber tHiS oNe, tHiS oNe WaS deep, darK, NaSty. I WaS beiNg cHaSed agaiN, by WHat I doN't KNoW. THrougH tHe tHicK OF a deNSe but dead For-eSt I raN..beiNg purSued by SoMe giaNt, treacHerouS, ugLy, FaNged, purpLe, MuSCLed 4-Legged beaSt

too many adjectives

Too bad...I tHougHt it WorKed

..........you seemed a lot smarter in your sleep...maybe you should have let that thing catch you this time.
No one cares about you here...you know that don't you?

And there she was, laying half naked on the futon, she was pretty despite the vomit.

God I Hope tHat iS HerS or SHe'S goNNa be piSSed.

Of course there is a 'her'.

But tHat'S tHe great tHiNg aboUt HeroiNe iSN't it? I SuppoSe drUgS iN geNeraL...I Have No idea WHooooooo tHiS
perSoN iS, bUt I StiLL to See tHe good partS oF Her (voMit
coVered or otHerWiSe) LayiNg iNCoHereNtLy oN My FUtoN...

yeah but since when do you have a futon?

YoU Stay oUt oF tHiS!

Oh shit you woke her up.

And with that he bolted back into his room, that
is...the room he woke up in...as it turns out this
wasn't his apartment.

Ha...I'M eveN StartiNg to act LiKe a drUggie

SHe iSN't Her. SHe iSN't My USUaL girL. Crap I caN Hear Her
MoViNg aroUNd.

He waits for screams from the discovery of
vomit but the only noise is the creaking of the
floor as she walks into the bathroom. No doors
close and water begins to run. He gathers a few ar-
ticles of clothing he wrongly assumes to be his (as
he is already fully clothed) and begins sneaking his

way towards the door. Down the hallway he creeps, tiptoeing, his eyes darting as he hears noises in other rooms. He stops in a nervous freeze as his stomach comes roaring to life. He is certain that everyone in the entire apartment building must have heard it's guttural cries and his ears pull his eyes to the left as he sees her...vomit girl...cleaning herself in a rusted moldy curtain-less shower. She noticed him and continued scrubbing without care or hesitation. He bolted for the door from fear of anyone recognizing him...he did not want to associate nor be associated with these people.

He had been slowly discovering the wares of the drug world and to his credit had fought to resist its temptations, even if momentarily.

He was formerly an upstanding citizen and a good, albeit entry level employee at a family-owned bank. He had been invited out several weeks ago by some old friends of his from high school...some riffraff he had the good sense to distance himself from after graduation. Several years had passed and he saw no harm in one night of catching up with the old gang. He pridefully boasted over a dinner feast of paper-wrapped value-menu burgers and cold beers about his job and his beautiful girlfriend, a curvy college student who worked as a part-time receptionist for a well-respected head shrink.

They smoked a bowl and laughed at the things that have changed over the years and talked about the things that have not.

Hours later he found himself watching as his friends shoved tiny spoons of powder up their nostrils. Not one to be called on account of cowardice, he soon found himself ignoring his inner voice and participating in the consumption of low-grade blow.

Since that night things had been spiraling out of control for the 20-something. His one-night introductory drug binge would eventually turn into a monthly, then weekly, then nearly daily occurrence. At first he had his circle of friends, the old riffraff that got him hooked, but he would go on to venture outside of that circle to score on his own and find himself in strange apartments with sexy vomit-covered women as he awakes from nightmares of being chased by very grotesque beasts.

This behavior was not something he could conceal and was becoming tired in his attempts to do so. His bank job had been lost and his savings depleted. He began lending himself to odd-jobs that initially bordered on illegal before becoming perverse and blatant in their illegality. His mental and physical well-being dwindled to nearly non-existent before the thought of addiction revealed itself to him that morning in that apartment with that woman and those terrible dreams. He had always struggled with his own inner voice which he believed to be his closest ally and moral compass...but lately that voice was becoming more and more irksome and disenchanted with the relationship.

Finding his way to the door he let himself out and began toward the stairs that would take him to the outside world and away from these people and that situation. He started to walk away from that door and toward the incredibly bright light of the new day. He recognized the sound of his shoes on the concrete floor of the building's hallway and understood in that moment that the clothes he had gathered in his arms belonged to someone else. With that revelation he scanned the hallway for any persons coming or going. Confident that he was alone he dropped the clothes where he stood and continued on his way to exit the building. He made his way down the three flights of stairs to reach the lobby of the apartment building. The brilliant morning sun beamed in through the doors and windows as if it had always been there.

A bright new day, there is no need to return to the darkness of these sorts of things.

Water First.

His whispered words did not go unnoticed and he lowered his head to avoid making eye contact with another man in the lobby who had been checking his mail. His gate increased as he made his way out the door into the fresh air.

Breathe. Try to remember your life before these things, before the drugs.

Quiet…Leave Me aLone.

It took the man a few city blocks to get his bearings. He figured a route home and put his feet on autopilot as he fought to recall the events that led him to that apartment the previous night. He was beginning to see what it was his inner voice had been warning him about over the last few weeks. He was beginning to see that he was no longer in danger of becoming a druggie...he was already there. He had liked to tell himself that so long as he remained judgemental toward the people he surrounded himself with he would remain above them, better than them, nothing at all like them. He had convinced himself that his was a recreational usage, he had ignored that obnoxious inner voice and had given in to every temptation that was offered.

He hated himself in those moments. He used to hate himself for what he was becoming and now hated himself for what he had become. The man wanted nothing more than to clean himself up and get back to the promising life that he had started with the bank and with his girlfriend. He wanted to get back on the straight—and—narrow and he was happy with himself for how genuinely he wanted that back. In spite of that fact, the worst was still to come for him, and it would take tragedy to shake him out of his cycle of destruction.

Two days had passed since waking up in that apartment and the familiar twinge of his addiction was starting to pain his joints and bones. He denied himself the satisfaction for as long as he could before succumbing to the early stages of withdrawal.

He knew what he needed and he knew how much it would cost and he knew he had no money.

Situations such as this one are what would lead him to those perverse and blatantly illegal acts that had been mentioned, acts that seemed to drive his inner voice even further into the stratosphere of high-and-mighty. Hearing that voice in his head condemn him for whatever it was he had to do to score was always just shy of being enough to make him quit. With a few dollars' worth of quarters in his pocket the man made his way to the corner pay phone and made a call to his usual provider. The man had no money and no credit with the dealer, so the dealer gave him the contact information of a man he knew who usually had 'a job or two' that needed to be taken care of for people seeking quick cash.

Within the hour the man found himself in the back of a vehicle with the clean-cut and suited man with a square jaw. He looked as though he had never touched an illegal substance in his life. He looked like someone who took care of himself and knew how good he looked in that suit, someone the man would not want to mix words with, someone who had a history of violence.

He had one job for the man, a relatively easy task of stealing a very specific vehicle and delivering it to a very specific location in the upcoming hours.

The man, more specifically his addiction, agreed to the terms of the job and was rewarded with a few quick bumps of coke to help him even out

before starting the job that would ensure his ability to afford his dependence for the next several
weeks.

Armed with the details of the upcoming heist
and a key to the SUV provided from the suit, the man
searched for a way to kill the nervousness building
inside of him until the hour arrived. He found his
way to the dilapidated house of one of his old high
school friends and drilled the heroine into his
veins; an advance from his friend in exchange for
some of the cash from the approaching theft and
the contact information of the suited-man that
paid cash for jobs.

The time had come to complete his task. The
man's friend dropped him off a blocks away from
location of the vehicle. The comfort of the drugs
still in his system calmed and reassured the man
that he had what it would take to complete the job,
his inner voice silenced, having given up on him for
the night.

He approached the location and found the vehicle, a black SUV. The man had no clue what was
special about this particular vehicle other than it
symbolized for him a bit of security in his continued inebriated existence. The key that had been
provided worked as promised and the man began
slowly down the street, having alarmed no one to
his presence.

He was to take the SUV to a drop point across
town, a 15 minute trip at most given the lack of
traffic in the early hours of that night.

The man drove in a paranoid silence as his current state of intoxication made focusing a bit more

difficult than he had anticipated. He fought to stay between the lines as his eyes would wander and images of that familiar beast would appear behind him, behind the vehicle, wanting again to chase him, to catch him, to end him.

The man knew from his previous encounters with the beast that it was not real, that this was a dream, a hallucination. That knowledge, however, was not enough to keep him from feeling the fear that comes from being chased. The man sunk down as far as he could into the leather seat and continually adjusted the rear-view mirror, searching and scanning for the monster. Anxiety weighed down the man's foot as the vehicle gained speed. The man had again found the beast behind him as it lunged toward the SUV. The man swerved to avoid the monster, the size and speed of the SUV made quick work of the parked car it tore through.

The jolt of the collision forced the man's hand down on the steering wheel and its momentum carried the vehicle over to its side, the passenger's door now toward the sky. The man pulled himself up through that door and gravity pulled him down face first to the grass as soon as he was out. He recovered to his feet and looked in horror at the carnage the beast had created. The man, now with an injured leg made it only a few blocks from the wreckage before the police found him.

It was that night and that wreck and the following rehabilitation that helped him to get clean and leave his addiction behind. Though there had been a passenger in the car he destroyed he had served minimal jail time as she had in one way or another survived the collision.

The man feared for a time the repercussions of failing to deliver the stolen SUV. He later found out from his friend who had provided him with the heroine that night in exchange for the suited-man's contact information that the suited-man had left town, returning to the mid-west to 'find his roots' or some such nonsense.

The man's inner voice did return to him in time and the man listened to that inner voice to guide him through the major decisions in his life. With the help of his inner voice the man successfully returned to a fruitful career and went on to marry his girlfriend the college student/receptionist. As he grew older and calmer he never lost the lessons of his more destructive, youthful days. His proudest achievement had been sobriety until his daughter and later his granddaughter were born.

Appendix 1

The Wreck

   We left the house and I began to
drive us around for a while before taking
her home. She sat there holding my hand and
whenever I would glance over at her I
could see happiness in her eyes, as if she
had been thinking about our future. Whatever
it was she was thinking it made her happy.
and the smile on her face was as beautiful as
any thing I had ever seen.
   We made our way down Childress Ave. to
a park and we sat in the car for a few
moments, quiet and happy. I knew as she did
that we _had_ to have each other, that we had
to be together + that the only way for us to
get through this life was next to one another.
   I leaned over to kiss her smile. She whispered
to me through that kiss what conceivably could be
the last words I will ever hear her say. I heard
her say my name, I heard her say she will
always love me and she will always be mine.
I said the same and asked if she would
get out and swing with me on the playground
as we had as children.

She moistened her lips with her tongue and nodded, I opened my door and got out. It was in those next moments that my melody ceased. The air around me had been displaced, sucked into the wake of a speeding SUV, bright lights rushed passed, followed only by the swift sounds of the confrontation.

I fell to my knees only to let out a whimper where a scream should have been. I picked myself up to my feet too quickly and stumbled light-headedly toward the debris of the crash. The SUV had ripped a gash through my car, there was nothing but blood and the smell of bodily fluids mixed with the fluids of the vehicles. I stumbled to the wreckage and found her covered in holes and cuts and blood. I reached for her as I began to yell for help, screaming so loudly and pulling air from the deepest reaches of my burning lungs that I began to lose consciousness. The darkness tunnelled my vision and I succumb to paralysis before giving in fully to darkness, to this misery

I woke up on my back, loaded into an ambulance, my arm pierced for some reason by an IV. I woke up staring at the lights above me through the salty blurriness of tears. I woke up to a man I did not know hovering over me, trying to ask me questions. At that moment my voice had been taken from me & I could not speak. I blinked & felt the warmth of tears and fear rush down the sides of my face. My mind raced as it never had before, knowing what I needed to ask, knowing that the one question I needed to ask was the one question I would never want to ask, and worse, that the answer to that question was the one answer I would never went to hear. I couldn't speak. I sat up quickly, arms bending and fists balling as they grabbed at the front of my hairline, tugging at my shirt, pulling out the IV from my left arm. I motioned forward in an attempt to pull myself out of the ambulance, only to be met by the hands of the EMT's sitting me back down on the gurney, reaching for straps. There was yelling and there was pointing and gaping. I needed so badly to see what was outside. I needed to look beyond the walls of that vehicle to see if the last thing I remember was real. I needed to see if she was there and if she was being taken care of. Through all of my fighting and struggling I had again been stuck, I was being sedated. I had never fought so hard to stay awake. I felt like I was sinking, drowning in my own eyes. The light tunnelled for a second time that night and I would not be awake again until the light of the following day shown through the windows of my hospital room. I was forced to leave my final night with her, I was thrust into this new day & into this new world in which she did not exist.

Appendix 2

Happy memory

She followed me up to my room and we lay in bed, my arms around her sobbing and jerking body and she unleashed a torrent of tears and snot on my shirt. I knew I had no promises to give, no rings or vows. I had only that moment, the moment we both existed in. All I could tell her with certainty is that I loved her and that I could never hold another person the way that I held her.

Hours passed by that night slowly, deliberately. As comfortable as we were together, as comforting as it was to have her next to me, there was something uncomfortable in that silence. There was nothing we could say without rehashing what we had already gone through. She knew I was hers and I knew she was mine. We grew up being a part of each other. I had no way of even knowing how to exist without her and her brother.

She turned to me, I was already facing her. Her eyes found mine. Her body followed and soon I was holding her next to me, pressed against me. As the distance between us closed I became increasingly aware of the events about to unfold. We kissed deeply and passionately as she realized what was happening to my body; her response was beyond compare. Her apparent level of provocation matched mine as she found her way on top of me, scrambling to undress.

There are several vivid images I remember from that night, so many incredibly intimate frames that flip through my mind. To me they are precious, near sacred + I hope to maintain that level of reverence for them as I put these words to the page.

I lay below her, her body hovering over mine, our hands intertwined as her lips ~~kiss~~ kiss mine. Her head disappears for a moment as I realize what is happening, as I realize we are sharing the same space. Her lips release from mine to give a soft moan so delicate that it could never be matched, but a moan so defined and perfect that I can hear it now, I can still feel her breath.

As her body became acclimated to mine I wrapped an arm around her and in one motion that matched the intensity of our kissing, we moved, her body now below mine. I held my weight with one arm as the other was free to grab at hers. She grabbed my hand and our fingers became as intertwined as our bodies in some sort of eternally sexy symmetry. Her free hand wrapped around the back of my neck, playing with my hairline.

We made love for the first time, our sweat melding and pooling above her navel, the base of her chest, or rolling off her body until finally we allowed ourselves to be pushed over the edge and into the chasm of our own satisfaction.

By 1 in the morning we were sitting up in bed making fun of how we had messed up each other's hair and beginning to mean the 'good nights' we started saying an hour and a half ago. It was so difficult to tear myself away from her. Even if it was just for a ~~~~ night, goodbyes could last for hours.

Appendix 3

Day 1

OK, here it goes. <u>Silence</u>... I didn't sleep very well last night. As dumb as it sounds once midnight rolled around I just laid there in bed, listening for my own voice to see if I would slip right away... as if my brain and my voice were two completely seperate entities.

She was there with me in my dreams last night but she did not speak to me. She stood there, I could see her clearly in front of me, gently swaying back and forth as if she were being softly moved by some calming breeze.

She has the most beautiful smile. She is my smile.

Day 2

I can't stop smiling! She spoke to me in my dream! It has worked! I hear her voice still in my mind, soothing and peaceful.

I miss her so badly but now I know that what I am doing will work... is working. I will go see her and sit with her this afternoon.

Staying silent... not speaking...it's a pain in the ass, especially when you are happy and excited.

Day 3

Another beautiful dream last night. There
still have been no changes at the hospital but
I believe she will come back to us soon.

It has only been two days, two full days
without talking. I am doing alright and
staying strong but I do catch myself
wanting to sing in my car, small things like
that. I am going to meet up with
Max this afternoon and then we are going to
see Mebdy.

The novelty of this challenge, this trial,
is already beginning to fade and I am
beginning to feel how difficult this
may become.

She was going to be my wife and
now I have all but lost her. I had fallen
so in love with this woman that I had
left little room in my heart for anything
else......

Day 4

Max's favorite new past time is trying to get me to break my silence. He farted in the car and locked the windows.

I contend that coughing, gagging and laughter are not violations of my silence.

I love him but I can't wait to see his face when she returns... I know it will happen.

Day 5

She held me last night and told me that she loves me.

Hearing her say those words... hearing her say say that she loves me is worth the hell of going through these past several months.

Nothing else is going well.

Last night I watched a movie with my folks. For a little while things felt normal. Mom got up to get something and asked if dad or I needed anything. Dad said 'no' and I smiled in appreciation and shook my head... she became emotional and did not return for a while.

I do feel guilt for what I am putting them through but my guilt over Melody outweighs all of it.

Mom knows I love her.

Day 6

Last night I held her and I told her I love her. In fact I told her that 'I love her to infinity one thousand times over.' I have never said those words to anyone but in my dream that is what came out. I guess it has a sweetness to it.

Today I am pulling myself out of my comfort zone and going out to dinner with my family. After that we will go visit Melody, other than that I have no clue what is going on.

--------- Part 2 ---------

I don't think there is a rule about writing twice in the same day. I was sitting next to Melody and a memory popped into my head.

Prom. Max and I really weren't into the idea of going to Prom but it was all Melody would talk about. Max asked a girl... Stacy ... she was a friend of Mel's. Mel had tried once or twice to bring in a friend from outside of our trio. Max and I never really let it happen. Typically it was some girly-girl that we would later find out only wanted

Still Day 6

to be friends with Melody because they had a crush on **Max**. Rarely was Max ever interested and so we would more often than not become very obnoxious to the new friend... never mean... just... obnoxious is a good fit.

Prom was a special occasion and Max played along and was nice to Stacy, I think this time Max's instincts as a brother kicked in when he saw Stacy's girly qualities fill Melody with excitement. The three of us (and Stacy) found ourselves heading to a diner, dressed to the 9's in the back of a limo.

It was Mrs. Black's perfume that sparked the memory. I could smell it as her mom walked into the hospital room today... it was the same perfume she always wore... the same perfume Melody wore to Prom... the same perfume she wore and tried to wash off the night she came home early from summer camp... The night of our first 'date'.

Tomorrow is time with Dr. Roberts.

Day 7

I wrote down a few thoughts for
Dr. Roberts about what this week has been
like for me, my family & friends.

He told me that it made sense for people
to feel isolated by what I am doing. Of
course I don't mean for this to be an act of
selfishness, but that is how it is being received.

He expects that before long people will
stop talking to me; not out of anger or hatred
but because they will become accustomed to
knowing I will not respond. Eventually they will
perceive my inability to speak as a desire to
simply be left alone.

His concern remains my mental well-being,
which many people are questioning. Doc assures
me he is looking for certain 'Hall marks,'
whatever that means.

He wants me back next week and to bring
my parents if we are all willing. I am up
for it.

Heading to the hospital to see her.

An Imperfect Fortress

Day 8

I sat with her again today. Melody just won't wake up.
I sit there... waiting... like every day... holding her hand and

scanning for movement... for any change at all... there are NONE.
I hold her limp hand + hope for some movement... praying for
some movement... dying for some movement.
I need rest... I have not slept well lately.

Day 9

I slept like 16 hours last
night. It very very needed.
I will eat tomorrow.
                    No dreams. . .

Nothing.

Day 10

I haven't slept naturally that much in a very long time. I ache today. I think it is from sleeping like that.

Time with Melody this afternoon, we'll see what happens.

I feel disconnected, probably from sleeping so long. There was no dream this time.

Between not ~~seeing~~ seeing her in my dreams & having no contact with anyone since binge sleeping, I feel very alone.

Day 11

Mom is upset. Dad keeps forgetting until I don't answer him, which is usually followed by some sort of 'Oh yeah' response.

I know they don't agree with any of this... my conviction is still there but I hate what is beginning to happen.

I hope she is there in my dreams tonight. For the most part things there are great. Here they are pensive and worrisome.

I hope this ends soon.

Come home, Mel.

Day 12

last night was different.
It used to be that we would speak.
I would speak, then her, then her or then me
or her then me, one thing or some other
thing or some other thing but last night
was nothing & I do not know what that
means. When I started this she would speak
but now her voice is gone.
I am trusting that everything will
be okay.

Day 13

Family day with Doc. Tomorrow...
time with Melody @ hospital today.

time alone tonight.

Day 141

Today my parents went with me to see Dr. Roberts. 5 minutes into the session they asked me to 'make an exception' & to at least talk while we were there. They don't see. They don't understand what that would cost, what that would negate. I will not lose my connection to her again.

While I was trying to listen to Dr. Roberts talk to my family I realized two (2) things:

① ~~It is becoming difficult~~

② It is becoming difficult to keep my attention on anything.

② I enjoy being around talking people.

There is something warm in feeling people talk, something you can not get from T.V.

To be in a small room with 3 (three) people for an hour was a nice break for me.

Day 15

My dream... she is there with some ONE new. There are no changes at the hospital.
  'She is still stable.'
Dammit there needs to be some change. change. change.

Wakeup wakeup wakeup wake up wakeup
                              Wake up

I know she can hear me.

I know she wants to come back...
    come back now please
  come home please
    I Need you.
      wake up

      come home

I need you

  to   Need

16

She was there again in my dreams last night. Again we said nothing... Something else is off. Seeing her is not enough... I need her to wake up. I need to tell her everything.

Something is changing...

Something has changed.
Something is different

/ the has

D 17

What the Fuck was I thinking?
How did we get here? I can not do
this alone. I know you can't either &
all I have wanted was to show you
that you don't have to be alone
& you don't have to go through it
alone... I am here for you but
you aren't responding to me. I
visit you everyday & I join
you every night, but now
you just stand there.
Now you bring **THAT**
with you... you bring
HIM with you.
Or **HER**, I can not
tell what **IT** is.

you bring **THAT** w/ you when I dream & I
do not know why.

WHAT is **THAT THING?**

Day 18

Enough laziness.   just speak
        speak to me.

                                    Do you know
He is growing   I am there
or you are   for you?
shrinking

          Today I
          need
          food.

        2 days is too (2) long
        I shake + I hurt.

Is It keeping
you? Is He
trapping you?
This
This Beast
you bring.

Day 19

Forgive me

20

There is nothing.

not ing ing ing i   ing   ing noting ing

ing ing   ing ing ing

not ing   not not not   not

ing ing ing ing   ing ing

not ing not not ing

there is nothing left.
there is nothing, right?

Day 21

There is concern. Dr. Roberts is worried now.
I gave him some impressions on paper & he
says I look shot... shaky & nervous.

My weight is down a bit & my clothes
fit a little differently... but his understanding
is extremely limited.

This is new territory for me as well but
I am in it. I am it & this is all that
is left. I know he can not understand
but he tries,... it is a waste. Thank you Doc.

If he were smart he would give up in
his attempts... like everyone does... If I
were smart I would abandon this, abandon
everything.

He wants me to go out... any where there
are people. He suggests The mall.

Day 22.

I understand, Doc. People, living & moving, speaking people, at the mall. Colors & voices & lights at the mall. No one I know, but it felt good. She was not there but neither was He. I still do not understand what IT is. When I see her, He is there. I think HE is what keeps her away. I think HE... IT is holding her captive. I think HE is the embodiment of her coma... I think she brings him when I dream. I think she is showing me that HE is what stands in the way before she comes back. IT must be stopped.

23

I stand no chance. I ~~[scribbled out]~~ Do not know how to beat It. It will not leave. It will not quit & It will not give her back to me. ~~He~~ won't let her speak. She is scared.

I am nothing. I am weak.

This will never stop

Day 24

It at times seems unbearable, the pain that comes with these memories. As happy, truly happy as those memories make me for that moment, they are fleeting & the reminder of the emptiness left in the wake lasts longer than I care for it to

But... I remember & I focus on these thoughts & these memories as if I am begging for both the happiness & the sorrow.

I will beg & I will pray for the pain to stop & I know that the only way that will ever happen would require that I forget completely these memories that warm me for that moment & that much I can not allow.

Day 25

I am going to the mall today to
~~xxxx~~ listen to the noises + sounds
     I need to buy new clothes
people make.
I am becoming a skeleton.

Food does not sound good + drink
                    seems pointless.

How could I let ~~xxxx~~ it get this far?

How did it get this bad?

     ~~It~~ can not be beaten

27

This is what time has meant.

I smile & I cry thinking about the many days & months & years that passed between that first moment & now.

I marvel at how quickly it has all happened. I pray & ask God to allow the clock to turn back to that exact instant so I could do it all again, it was the moment my life began. What I would give to be there again. Smiling & full of hope. I miss her, I miss the moment & I miss the great & wonderful things she made me feel. This memory is just one of ten thousand that swim in my brain, only a small taste of the beauty & the pain.

28

I see faces that remind me of ~~[scribbled out]~~ you from time to time. I stop & I look & I know that they are not you & I become at them for it... angry that they are walking & smiling & talking & living & that they are not you & that they remind me of you & angry that they have stolen some feature that reminds me in some way of you & how you look & who you are & I am angry.

No Dr. today
Need sleep.

Night 29

I can not sleep. Sun will be up soon but now everything is dark. Even my heartbeat disappears after a few still moments.

She remains silent behind her **BEAST**

Dreams are more desolate.

Tomorrow I will sit with Melody again... as I always do.
I will hold her hand & seek peace.

30

I no longer recognize what I am dreaming. Her Beast has grown larger & overtaken everything.

Every night I search & scramble, watching & quietly waiting. ~~/////~~

The visions of HIM follow me throughout the day. The thoughts I ~~have~~ have are no longer my own They are HIM, they will not stop. stop

What am I doing?
    What justice is there in suffering?

HE cannot Be
    Destroyed.

Day 31

I miss ~~her~~ her every moment. I miss her every movement.

There is nothing powerful left in me.

I am surrounded by people who live in hope. There is no connection.

no relation or kinship.

Just unshakable apathy.

They are not like her, they are full of life + now It has her + will not give her up She is all but dead.

That feels like an eternity ago.

Every day is it's own eternity.

The pain + the lonely feel fresh + new everyday as though a scab has been peeled off every I look into my dreams.

There can be no such scab, no callous, no scar for

This   wound.

This wound will bleed a blood that will never run out.

32

I am lost in the dark of this
silence.

I am lead & guided only by
the idea of a woman who has changed
the course of my life... & even though
I can not truly see her without
close my eyes...
She gives me sight.

33

Melody,

There is so much to say but nothing I could say even if I wanted to. I want to grab you & shake you & tell you to open your eyes, those beautiful eyes, & look at me. I need you to see me in front of you. It has been so long since you left. It feels like ~~a lifetime~~ since I told you that I am in love with you.

I am in love with you Melody. I am begging, I am pleading.

I can think only of our past & hope for glimpses into the future... so far no such glimpse has come to me.

You stay strong.
I am trying.

I love you

www.ingramcontent.com/pod-product-compliance
Lightning Source LLC
Chambersburg PA
CBHW050424260626
47156CB00003B/1147